Adventures in
Black & White
Short Stories & Poems

2016-2017 Beaverlodge
Regional High School Students

Beaverlodge, Alberta, Canada

Book Cover Designed by: Kaitlynn Sperling

WE HAD A CONTEST IN BOTH SEMESTER 1 & 2
WE ASKED STUDENTS FOR ENTRIES OF POEMS
AND SHORT STORIES – THIS BOOK IS THE
RESULT…

LET THE ADVENTURES BEGIN…..

ACKNOWLEDGMENTS

We would like to thank everyone at Beaverlodge
Regional High School for their part in making this
book a reality. From the students who entered the
contest, to the teachers and staff who read and
judged the entries, to Ms. Troskot's attention to
detail and Kaitlynn Sperling who created such an
awesome book cover.

CONTENTS

"A Reader Lives A Thousand
Lives Before He Dies.
The Man Who Never Reads
Lives Only One"

George R.R. Martin

Winning Entries
2016 – Semester 1
Short Stories:

First Place - Kennedy Langlois – *The Rainbow Beach*
Second Place – Josie Kjemhus - *Calvin*
Third Place – Belle Vetsch - *Forbidden Practices*

Poems:

First Place – Tate Cook – *In The Midnight Glade*
Second Place – Tassi Jarvorsky – *Life*
Third Place – Lacey Bryden-Reid – *On Halloween*

2017 –Semester 2
Short Stories:

First Place – Josie Kjemhus – *Symbol of Pain, Monster Within*
Second Place – Tassi Jarvorsky – *Promises Under Umbrellas*
Third Place – Nevada Alde – *Resilience*
Honorable Mention: Kisikaw Rogers – *Red Ink*
Layton Guise - *Dust*

Poems:

First Place – Kennedy Langlois – *Never Forgotten*
Second Place – Emily Melville - *Clouds*

1ST PLACE SHORT STORY (SEMESTER 1)
THE RAINBOW BEACH
BY: KENNEDY LANGLOIS

The dirty brown water washed up onto the shore in the form of a tired wave, and as it receded it left behind remnants of a world forgotten. In the dusty sunshine that shone through the smog, the gravel glittered like gemstones. Theodore imagined that if there was anything natural and beautiful in the world, it was the rainbow colored shards that made up the beach. But Papa told him once that it hadn't always been this way.

That this precious beauty was not natural at all.

He had said that instead of the gemstone gravel, there had been something called sand, and that it had been warm and golden in the sunshine, and that you could take your shoes off and wiggle your toes through the tiny grains. After hearing that Theodore ran back to the beach and threw his shoes off, only to be horrified at the tiny cuts and bits of metal stuck in the soft skin of his young feet. He had hobbled home, whimpering in pain.

As the smell of the acidic ocean forces its way into Theodore's nose, he is reminded of the time that Papa had said the air was once sweet and cool, and that people could go outside without having to lug around oxygen tanks on their backs. He said that when he was a boy, oxygen tanks were only for sick people. Dying people.

Theodore takes a small step towards the soupy surf until the toes of his shoes rest against the foam. His eyes scan the beach, watching and waiting for the moment he would have to race back to the safety of the higher ground, out of the wave's reaching fingers.

It was Theodore and his little sister Madeline's favorite game, but for now, he was playing by himself. Maddy had always had trouble breathing, even inside with the imported mountain air, and one night Mother and Father had come to him crying, saying they had to send Maddy away, and she wasn't coming back. But Theodore knew that one day she would come back and they could once again play at the beach.

At that moment the murky water rushes forward faster than he expects and seeps through his shoes, burning his tender feet. Theodore gasps and bounds back to the upper beach, sucking in shallow breaths as he waits for the stinging and burning to subside. He would have to get Mother to bandage his feet, and listen to her grumble to his father about his dangerous games. Then once she was finished and her back was turned, he would race back to the beach on his chipped blue bicycle.

He would travel through the shell of a city to his beach. The acrid air would sting his face and when he once again arrived he would stare out at the expanse of chocolate milk colored sky and sea.

Papa told him once that the sky used to be blue, and Father told him to stop telling tall tales. Papa only grumbled and pulled Theo onto his broad lap, telling him how people used to not only touch the water but swim in it as well. That was Theodore's favorite tale of them all.

The idea that you could dive into water — much like the stuff he bathed in — and swim without melting down to bones, was utterly insane to him. It had to be a made up story.

***

Papa said that there used to be things in the water, things that were alive, that swam, that you could eat, and that could eat you. Now that was a tale. Theo had laughed at him and his Papa had sworn it to be the truth, and in his frustration ranted that there used to be alive things that could fly and slither and run, big things and small things, and whole areas where only these things lived. These things were wild and better and smarter than people.

Mother from her spot on the couch shushed him. Theodore giggled about that too.

"You shouldn't speak of such things as fact," she scolded Papa. She told Theodore that Papa had false memories and that he wasn't in his right state of mind.

"Tell me, Lorraine, how do you explain all of the proof that litters our Museums? Tell me why an animal would destroy its home," Papa grunts in response. His wrinkle creased eyes shine with anger, and Theo could not help but notice the flash of wisdom deep under the surface. He shook it off.

"Wild animals are creatures of fiction Michael, and if they existed they probably wouldn't destroy their home," Mother replied.

"Mankind once believed that we stemmed from a humanlike animal, and it was a thought that wasn't looked at with disgust," the old man retorted.

"Listen, Michael, these animals you speak of, were only a hoax created by the government, much like the Moon Landings and the idea of global warming," Theodore's mother chortled. Theodore joined in.

"Look around would ya! We destroyed this world!" Papa snapped. His breaths had become labored in his hysteria.

Father looked up from his news tablet at the sharp tone of Papa's voice. "Enough, this isn't something to discuss in front of young ears," Father answered. Theodore had jumped down from his

Papa's lap and smiled sweetly at his mother. He could help his grandfather feel better.

"Mother I think it's time for Papa's nap," he suggested. His mother had given him a half smile before nodding.

"I think you're right," she agreed. She had stood up and circled his wheelchair as if he was one of the wild animals he had talked about. Papa grumbled about being treated like a child as he was wheeled away, and Mother told him to stop acting like one in response.

Theodore had then returned to his beach to play with the shards of rainbow gravel.

***

Theodore, his feet stinging with every step, limps his way up the rainbow beach to his bicycle that leans against an old rotted post. He walks the bicycle off the yellowed grass and onto the cracked pavement. He then hops onto the seat and rests his aching feet onto the pedal and with a kick of his foot he rides through the broken streets until he reaches the crisp, clean ones.

When he reaches his concrete house and hobbles inside, tears leak from his eyes and snot drips from his nose. He wipes his face on his striped t-shirt, leaving sopping wet spots.

When his mother sees him, she flies into a rage of worry and anger. She grabs ointments and wraps and sets to work bandaging the burns and sores littering his feet; Theodore sits still, letting her fuss over him. Theo can hear his Father and Papa grumbling about acid rain, and having to recoat the acid shield to the house again. It had rained more this year than any, and Theodore's father would have to coat the house in an acid protectant, so it would not eat away the roof over their heads.

When his mother is finished with Theo she helps him into the sitting room and into a chair beside his Papa. As Theo waits for the stinging in his feet to subside, he and his Papa watch the sky slowly begin to dribble. Then the dribble turns into a mess of acidic water and ash, and the puddles outside turn soupy.

"When I was a boy we played in the rain, danced and laughed and let it drip onto our tongues. If you were to do that now you would melt yourself from the inside out," he mutters. Theodore turns to him.

"Papa, will you tell me a tall tale? The one about the alive things in the ocean?" Theodore asks politely.

His grandfather glares at him. "All that I tell you is fact, history. It is imbeciles like your father and mother who choose not to believe it."

He shoots one of his glares at Theo's father sitting on his couch; his father shakes his head in annoyance. Theo's grandfather turns back to him.

"Listen Theo, I'll tell you more about history when you're ready for it. When you're ready to believe and accept it," Papa finishes and turns back to glaring out the window at the acid rain that falls relentlessly.

For the next two years, Theodore visits the rainbow beach religiously. Even in his dreams, he sits on the colorful beach that no one else can bare to look at. He watches as the waves slosh up against the sharp gravel, and moan back into the disgusting sludge that is the ocean. Yet the rainbow beach never stops being beautiful, never stops amazing him. And not once does he stop to imagine what it could have been.

What it should have been.

After growing tired of playing alone, Theodore tries to persuade other boys and girls to join him when his sister still does not return but the others say their parents will not allow them near the rainbow beach. But the other children beg him each day to bring them shards of the gemstone colored gravel, they make their specific color requests and he obliges with a smile the size of the moon. He then spends hours sifting through thousands of shards, looking for the perfect color. In his mind he was a miner, searching for the perfect gemstone, one that would make him rich beyond his wildest dreams.

But soon even that grew dull, and all he could do to pass time was watch the foggy sunshine dance lazily across the shard beach.

***

The first day he started coughing and wheezing was the day his parents forbid him from going back to the rainbow beach. His tears fell like the acid rain that night, burning his face while they rolled over his chubby cheeks. His mother held him tight that night, and all the nights that came after when coughing fits left blood in the palms of his hands.

Still, he visited the rainbow beach in his dreams, yet it grew duller each night and disappeared altogether the first morning he could not suck in enough air to get out of bed.

That was the day he was hooked up to an oxygen tank while he was inside his home, surrounded by the expensive imported mountain air. He could hear his mother crying in her bedroom at night when his coughing and hacking woke her, and his father soothing her with quiet words that he could not hear. During the days all he could do was watch the acid rain slip hungrily down the window sill, searching for something else to destroy in its wake as his mother read him facts about the food industry. He always pretended to be interested.

Then one day he could not sit up.

His mother squeezed her fingers until they were whiter than her young son's face, whiter than the pristine house they lived in.

"Mother, can you send Papa in to see me please?" Theodore wheezed his request. His mother nodded through barely contained tears and left the room, his grandfather returned in her place. Theo's grandfather rolled up quietly beside the bed before reaching out and taking Theo's hand. "Papa, I'm ready," Theo gasped out. And by some miracle his grandfather understood. His eyes shone with tears as he gazed down at Theo, a small joyless smile on his lips.

"Now Theo, history is an ugly thing and while some believe it to be fake, the truth and proof are all around us. Mankind as a whole destroyed our planet, our home. We took too much, too often, and didn't give the Earth enough back. Our greed destroyed the oceans, the forests, even the air. We wasted our food sources, slaughtered all the animals, and then began slaughtering each other. We dumped our waste and garbage into the oceans and let the fish go belly up. We cut the forests down. We poisoned the air with smoke so choking black that it blocked the sun out for days on end. And at the end of it all, when there was nothing left, we realized what we had done, and that it could never be fixed, not in a thousand lifetimes.

The people today like to delude themselves into believing a lie, one so blatantly obvious, because they are embarrassed," his wise crinkled eyes find Theo's muted gray one, "your rainbow beach is a cold, hard reminder for our failure as a species of Earth, a reminder of our greed, our inadequacy." His eyes drift away from Theo's as he finishes. But he turns his wrinkled face back to Theo's sick one, a smile plastered on his lips, but it does not reach his watery gray eyes.

"Quite a tale hey?" he forces a breathy laugh, one that could turn into sobs any second. He knew his grandson believed him, every single word believed to be the truth, something no one had ever done.

"Thanks, Papa," Theo smiles weakly. His grandfather nods and pats his grandson's small pale hand then rolls his chair out of the room. Theo nods to himself, the small movement sending shooting pain down his spine. A headache blooms through his skull and he moans, and then bursts into a violent coughing fit. His mother bursts into a fresh round of tears from the other room.

The neighborhood kids come by to see Theodore, each bringing their gravel shards from the rainbow beach, they pile them on his bedside table. Theodore smiles, but no joy fills him at the sight of the shards.

After brief goodbyes are murmured Theodore's mother ushers them out of the room and thanks them all for coming, her voice is strained. His father sits beside his bed in a chair and rests his forehead against the bed sheets, exhaustion weighs his shoulders down. When Theo's mother returns he smiles at her, then taps his father's forehead. They both look at him, expectant.

"I would — like to — go — to sleep," Theo gasps out.

They look at each other and nod, then take turns kissing his damp forehead.

"We'll just be in the next room if you need anything baby," his mother says.

Theo nods, "tell — Papa I love — him."

His mother nods again and shuts the door behind her.

Relief pools into Theodore's stomach once they are gone, they take their sorrow with them. Theodore smiles softly and exhaustion slows his ragged breathing and pulls his eyelids down. Sleep overcomes him easily, and with it, the image of his rainbow beach dances behind his tired eyes. But it's different.

Strange, yet familiar.

His face is warm.

He breathes in the air that is clean, air that tastes sweet on his tongue. The brown sky fades into a cloudless blue, the sludgy water changes into

flowing liquid the color of turquoise and he
watches as the rainbow shard beach slowly
disappears, leaving behind the warm sand.

Sand that sparkles like stars in the dark.

Sand that is a radiant gold in the sunlight.

It was the most beautiful thing he had ever seen.

2ND PLACE SHORT STORY (SEMESTER 1)
CALVIN
BY: JOSIE KJEMHUS

Cheers erupted and filled the room. Screaming in excitement, I turn around and kiss my husband, Justin. I cry in his arms as our families and closest friends surround us in a group hug. Blue balloons reached the ceiling, and across them was the words "It's a boy!" I am overcome with joy thinking about the change to come in three months, having a baby son.

We celebrated until the sky went dark. Our new acreage was only a five minute drive away. As we travel home, the ride feels strenuous for a tired pregnant woman.

"It doesn't seem real. Even though I feel the baby-him every day, it just seems like a dream," I grab Justin's hand.

"Well it'll sink in when you feel like you are pushing a watermelon out of your-"

"Hey! Quit it!" We burst out laughing. Rain sprayed the windshield, causing a mist to hover over the highway.

"Justin, turn on the high beams, it's really hard to see tonight..." I let go of his hand to reach the defrost button for him. Anxiously, I kept an eye on the ditches. This was the worst road for wildlife. I wait, the high beams are still not activated.

"There's wildlife honey, please turn up the head--- Justin! There's a moose!" It was too late. Suddenly, we are showered with broken glass. Our truck swung to the left and hit a patch of ice. The moose tumbled from the hood and swung above us. Before I knew it, we are upside down, resting in the ditch. I couldn't move. The seatbelt was digging into my stomach, making it hard to breathe. Immediately I scream at Justin to save our baby.

"Sarah? Baby, stay still. We're okay, I'll get you unstuck." Justin turns off the engine, unbuckles his seatbelt and falls to the hood of the truck. My husband's hands wrap around my body as he struggles to get me out of my seatbelt.

Tears start to roll from my bleary vision. Repeatedly, I asked Justin, "Is the baby okay? Will he be okay?" Slowly, my eyelids droop and I feel my body fall into the arms of my husband.

***

"Sarah, we are at the hospital. Please wake up, you're okay," an unfamiliar voice wakes me up. Confused, I attempt to sit up but hands restrain me from doing so. As I open my eyes, I see Justin's face inches from mine, feeling his lips touch my forehead. I groan, racking my brain to remember what is going on. Thoughts flood my mind, and I begin to remember everything.

"Is he okay Justin? Is he dead?" exhausted sobs pour from my body. Leaning over, I collapse into his arms. If I am in the hospital, it must mean I lost the baby.

"Our baby is perfectly okay. As soon as the ambulance dropped you off here, they performed an ultrasound to assure the baby wasn't affected by the crash. All three of us are safe. Fortunately, you and I are just cut up from the broken glass. The doctor said you may have blacked out from a minor concussion. Other than that, we made it okay."

"Can we go home?" my voice cracks.

"Yes, I'll help you get dressed. Your mom is on her way to take us home." Justin sits me up and wipes my eyes. The clock read 1:22 am, and all I want to do was go home to my own bed.

***

 The next morning I fight to open my eyes, let alone get out of bed. My back throbs and I feel a jolt of pain in my left temple. Struggling, I stand up and wrap my white bathrobe around my tender body. The sun beams so vividly into my sensitive eyes as I look out the window. It is a quiet day, with the wind tickling the pine trees. I recollect the events that occurred last night. My hands hold my belly, feeling grateful that our baby boy is okay. Slowly, the door opens with a soft creaking sound. Justin walks in as something catches my eye across the field.

"The doctor ordered bed rest, Sarah. How are you feeling?" He joins me at the window.

"There's something out in the field over there. Do you see it?" A small animal is crossing the field. The dark tan figure has skinny, horse-like legs, and a long muzzle.

"Is that a foal?" Justin questions. There are no horses around our acreage so the idea seems bizarre.

"Weird, it looks like a baby moose without a-" Rapidly, I put two and two together, and realized the absence of its mother. "You don't think it was the baby's mother we killed last night, do you?" Guilt fills my stomach with nausea.

Justin and I jump into my car and drive past our overturned truck. Ravens surround the road kill, pecking at its flesh. I step out of my car and looked around for signs of a calf. Without fail, Justin found what we were looking for. As we guessed, the tracks in the snow showed the mother's tracks, and beside them were smaller, innocent hoof prints.

"She did have a baby… We have to do something. Do we notify the Police or Fish and

Wildlife?" I reach into my pocket for my cellphone, but Justin stops me.

"Fish and Wildlife will just relocate him. Do you remember when my family raised a baby deer in our barn? My brother found it freezing near the creek and assuming something happened the mother, we took it in. Once it was old enough, it wandered off, but stuck around to come back for oats and hay."

"Justin, if you're thinking about taking the baby moose home, what will we feed him until he can eat hay?" We sit down in the car.

"My father fed the fawn cow milk for the first month. Eventually we gave him oats." he turns on the engine and starts driving home.

"Will the calf stay in the barn? We can't leave him to die."

"At the moment, the calf is in the cattle fence. Most likely it'll be skittish, but I will try to get ahold of him. But you have to go back to bed as soon as we're home," he looks at me with concern. No energy to argue, we drive home in silence.

After I eat some chicken soup, I go upstairs to sleep, with Joey, my golden retriever puppy trailing close behind me. Unintentionally, I fall asleep and wake up half a day later. The sun was setting, and a golden red color is shining through my window, spilling the color over my white walls. Joey licks my hand as I sit up. I decide to check on

Justin, thinking about the possibility that he caught the calf.

Bundling up in a winter coat, scarf and gloves, I step out onto the porch. As I turn the corner around the house, I see Justin bottle feeding the little moose out in front of the barn.

Noticing me walking towards them, Justin shouts from across the yard, "Sarah, he's a boy! He looks like a Calvin to me!" I can see his smile already.

I greet the baby, so-called Calvin. His doe-like ears perk up, and his stance tightens with nerves. I reassure Calvin that I won't hurt him, and he begins to warm up to me. Justin hands me the bottle of cow milk, which I realize was all that was available to us.

Calvin sucks on the bottle, creating a vile slurping sound. His head jerks back and forth and I can't help but giggle to myself.

***

Weeks go by, and Justin and I have decided to keep Calvin around.

Quickly, I learned that when you have a baby moose, the farm becomes very popular with visitors. Parents around Valhalla were bringing their children to bottle feed the neighbor's moose. Most certainly, a Canadian way to spend one's Saturday evening.

Calvin and Joey have become friends. The calf and puppy are inseparable. Due to the constant bellowing we hear at nightfall, Calvin has been promoted from the barn to the porch of our house. He is spending the majority of his time cuddling our dog.

Our friends came over from down the road, and brought their two young boys, Tyler and Jesse. Instantly, Calvin bonded with the two boys. Tyler and Jesse would run around our house and the three foot moose would come bounding behind them.

"What are you and Justin going to do when he grows much taller and…" Joanne, the mother of the boys paused. "I'm just worried that's all."

"Trust me, I know what you mean. We shouldn't get attached to a wild animal, but he doesn't know how to survive out there. Where else would he go if we called someone to take him away? I don't know what to say, or who to ask." I look at Justin for reassurance, but he shrugs his shoulders.

"Have you researched about moose behavior?" Joanne's husband, Tim questions.

"No, but…" I was interrupted.

"When we go into the bush to load the logs, we have encountered violent moose before. My buddy and I were tightening the wrappers of our log trailer when the boss called an emergency stop. I looked to my right and a bull moose, taller than a pickup truck, was galloping towards me. I lunged under the load to get away. He nearly nicked my buddy, Alan. The bull paced around our semis for about fifteen minutes, only pausing to paw the muddy road. Let me tell you, moose ain't no fun and games, Sarah. What you are doing is a dangerous thing," Tim rubbed his jaw. "Sarah, you are a dental assistant. Not a forest ranger."

My hand covered my mouth. An overwhelming sense of dread pounded over me. Deep down, I knew Tim had good intentions, but anger swelled up inside me. Calvin was as innocent as his two boys, and I tell myself that he will always stay that way.

***

Calvin is three months old now. He sleeps on our porch, and eats from the bucket of oats and hay beside the barn. Life has started to return back to normal, and leaving the calf for work has become easier.

Friends and family we have told adapted to Calvin being a part of our family. The families who live on our road are really supportive about it. The crazy neighbors who have a pet moose has become the new normal in this small town.

Justin hands me a cup of coffee. Being nine months pregnant, I struggle to gain the energy to do such mundane tasks. My body is so exhausted, and ready for this baby to come and meet us.

"The baby could come anytime, Sarah. Are you excited?" He grabs my hand from across the oak dining table.

"Realistically, I'm nervous. Although, I just want to get the birth over with. My body hurts."

"Think of it this way, we are well prepared. The nursery is furnished and decorated, we have all the materials we need and the hospital bag is packed. Soon enough, he'll be here."

That very night, while watching a movie, my water broke. Intense contractions came without hesitation. By the time we arrived at the hospital, I was dilated eight centimeters, and it wasn't long before I had to begin pushing. Justin stayed by my side the entire time and held my hand. Forty-five minutes later, our son was born.

Laying in the hospital bed, I held our baby son, Troye Werner. His blonde hair created miniature curls, originated from his father's genes. His chubby face glowed with joy, and his beautiful blue eyes beamed with curiosity. My parents and in-laws sat around me, taking turns holding the baby. A sensation of joy, pride and relief hit me like a tidal wave. Tomorrow, my husband and I will be taking home a healthy, happy boy.

Justin was a nervous wreck driving home from the hospital. He was paranoid, and developed a small case of road rage.

"Why are you so close behind me? Back off!" the car horn went off. Surprisingly, Troye slept the entire hour drive home. Playfully, I laughed at my husband and assured him that we will be okay.

Justin carries Troye up to the nursery with me. A waft of lavender filled the room as I open the door. The baby blue walls breathed a sense of comfort to me. Troye's room is decorated with white furniture, supported with a white leather recliner, cute paintings of elephants, a fuzzy blue rug, and a coffee table with a selection of children's books under a white polar bear stuffed animal. Leaning over the crib, Justin lays Troye down for a nap.

Through the corner of my eye, I see Calvin playing with Joey out in the field, chasing each other. Smiling, I gain Justin's attention, and take a moment to watch our other two babies play freely. Opening my phone, I take a picture of them. Unexpectedly, an overwhelming sense of joy hit me, thinking about the life I have. My eyes began to droop, and I tell Justin that I love him. The white recliner was calling my name, so I sit down and slowly fall asleep.

As I was breastfeeding Troye in the living room, the doorbell rings. Not expecting anybody on a Sunday morning, I call Justin from the kitchen to see who it is. I overhear the conversation between Justin and a man who sounded official.

"Good morning. Is this Mr. Werther?" the stranger greets Justin.

"Yes, can I help you?"

"I am Officer Eric, from Fish and Wildlife. Recently, we have been notified of the containment of a young moose. Is that correct?" My stomach drops.

Justin laughs, "You're mistaken, Officer. My wife and I are not containing a moose. There is a calf that is sticking around, but he has free range and we have no responsibility over him."

"That is not what we have been told. I am here to let you know that under the Wildlife Act of Alberta, Canada, it is illegal to contain any wildlife without a permit or license. If this situation is not taken care of, we will have to put matters into our own hands." The officer flips through his notebook.

"The moose is not contained in any way, sir. You have no reason to be concerned," Justin is trying not to get angry.

"Then I suggest you start scaring him away, and quit providing food if that's the case. It is not safe for a moose to be close to farms, with no fear of humans. When that bull grows up, he will not be a friendly face. You have two weeks until our next visit. Have a good day sir, say hi to your wife for me." The door shuts, and I begin crying.

After the officer left, Justin joined me on the couch. We sat in silence for a very long time. Troye started to let out a cry, so Justin took him from me and started to burp him.

"What are we going to do?" I look at Justin for a comforting answer.

"Sarah, we are going to continue exactly what we have been doing this whole time. Realistically, we are not breaking any laws."

***

Rain splattered the windows and the dirt was fashioned into a muddy slush. Calvin and Joey took shelter on the porch and we spent the day relaxing inside the house. The sky was a dreary grey with very little sunlight. Waiting for my husband to return home from getting some groceries for supper, I watch a Disney movie. Just as the pumpkin turns into the carriage, the front door opens.

"Hey Miss Sarah and Troye boy! Lasagna is on the menu tonight!" Justin rubs his hands together and blows his warm breath on them. Plopping down beside me, he wraps his arms around my shoulders and kisses Troye's forehead.

"Did you notice anything strange with Calvin? He was laying down when I left, and he's still on his side." Justin informs me.

"Oh, I haven't been outside yet. I assumed he was just cold in this weather." I shot him a questioning look. Concerned, I stood up and looked out the window. Calvin's long legs were stretched out, and his breathing was exaggerated. "Is it what we are feeding him?"

"We will keep an eye on him, if he's not better tomorrow, I will figure something out."

For the next few days, Calvin's behavior changed drastically. Joey and Calvin no longer played as much, and the moose spent all of his time sleeping in the shade of the porch.

I begin to worry about Calvin's reliability on us. In a week's time, the Fish and Wildlife Officer will return and expect a different situation. Our moose is still close to our home, and I am not sure that will change anytime soon.

***

My brother Nick lives six hours away. Growing up, he was always the overachiever that impressed my parents, only making me the letdown. He became a surgeon in the city of Edmonton, and I only developed into a dental assistant in a small town of Beaverlodge. I married a farmer, he married a plastic Barbie.

His visits only seem to remind me that my opinions and decisions seem to always fall below his. In this particular situation, I was neck deep in worry. Nick was coming to visit his nephew, who just turned a month old. Not only was I adapting to life as a mother, I was living with a moose taller than myself...

I take a sip out of my morning coffee, and look out our picture window. A shiny, black Camaro pulls into the driveway. My stomach dives, knowing Calvin is waiting on the porch to greet him.

"Sarah! There's a moose on your porch! Should I get some help?" Nick shouts from his car window.

Shock appears on his face as I open the door, and step out beside Calvin. The little sister attitude got to me, as I put my hand on the animal's back and smiled suspiciously.

"This is your second nephew, Calvin." The statement couldn't be blunter. Justin joins beside me, holding Troye. Bursting out laughing, I wave Nick to come inside. Confused, he doesn't say a word until we close the door to the kitchen.

"What in the world is THAT? Do you realize how dangerous he is?" My brother elevates his tone of voice.

"Let me explain, Nicholas," I felt the courage to stick up for myself, "Justin and I got into a bad accident almost two months ago. We killed the mother moose and found her baby the next day."

"Why wasn't I told about this?" Anger rose in his voice.

"Justin and I don't owe you any explanation as to why we have a moose hanging around. We aren't containing him, and we aren't breaking any laws. Can you just spend some time with Troye? It's the only reason you drove out here." My patience was lost. I storm to the other side of the kitchen to grab my cold coffee. Justin remains silent.

"To be clear, I was going to offer a babysitting shift tonight so you two could go out and spend some time outside of this farm. Dress up, I don't care. Just get out of the house and I will spend some one on one time with my nephew." Nick offers with frustration.

Justin convinced me that we needed a night out, and I knew we did. Although it wasn't the first time leaving Troye with someone else, the thought still made me sweat.

We sit in the car and I adjust my red blouse. In the visor mirror, I make sure my hair and makeup looks presentable. Tonight was the first night in months that we have gone out on a date, and I wanted to look pretty.

"Sarah, you look striking. There is no reason to be tense. Your brother is a surgeon, not a criminal."

The joke didn't make me laugh. I turn on the radio to kill the silence and enjoy some country music.

After the movie, we went to a fancy supper. Justin impressed me with how he dressed, and his formality. After all, farmers are the best gentlemen.

The drive home took an hour. As we pull into the driveway, I see an unfamiliar truck sitting in front of the house. The headlights illuminated the garage doors, showing a silhouette of a man in front of it.

"Who would be here this late at night?" Justin utters as he steps out of the car. Waiting, I grab my phone to call Nick, but Justin hurries back to the car. Anxiety fills my stomach as I ask, "What's wrong? Who is that? Is Nick inside?"

As soon as I look to my right, I saw Nick assisting a man with loading game into the back of the stranger's truck. Heaving the animal, and it lands with a thumping sound. A pink tongue hangs out of the mouth, with doe like ears flopping to the side…

"Sarah, I think you should go inside…" Justin wouldn't make eye contact with me. Slowly, my thoughts, like puzzle pieces, are fitting together.

"That can't be ---"

"Go inside Sarah, please. I need to handle this." Justin interrupts sternly.

"Handle what? Oh my… Is that Calvin, Justin? Did Nick shoot Calvin?" I began to cry.

Nick paces on the front porch. "I apologize. A man knocked on the door around six thirty, and asked for permission to hunt on your acreage. Assuming Calvin was safe, I gave permission, just like you would have," my brother admits. Morning sun beats down on our faces and melts the snow. Joey wouldn't leave the blood still stained on the ground where Calvin laid.

"You are a liar. How gullible do you have to be, to believe Calvin, a bull moose, wouldn't be killed? Nick, you gave the hunter permission on purpose! You thought we couldn't handle him!" my voice raises. "I trusted you with my baby, and you allow my animal to be shot!"

"That moose was not your animal! He had free range. Be thankful, you don't have to deal with him anymore." Nick approaches me, but I back away.

"Get off my property, right now." I demand. Anger boils in my chest and chases the tears away. Thankfully, Justin walks out of the house and nods in agreement. Swiftly, the black Camaro leaves the farm and the baby monitor screams for our attention.

***

"Mommy, why is there a picture of a moose on the wall?" Troye asks curiously. Six year olds never run out of questions.

36

"Your father and I rescued a baby moose, right before you were born." I reply. Interestingly, I haven't talked about Calvin in years.

Troye sat down on his striped bean bag chair. Looking up with his ocean blue eyes, he says, "Can you tell me more? What happened to him?"

"Alright." I sit down on the floor beside him. "The moose was named Calvin, and we fed him oats and hay so he would stay around. Do you remember our old dog Joey? He was very close friends with Calvin, they played all the time, like the picture up there." I point to a second photo.

"Where is he, Mom?"

My voice cracks as I answer, "He wandered off one day, and never came back home."

"Did he find a family?" Troye questions.

"I'm sure he is running around in the snow, playing with his friends right now..." a tear falls from my eye.

3RD PLACE SHORT STORY
(SEMESTER 1)
FORBIDDEN PRACTICES
BY: BELLE VETSCH

A bold knock at the door catches my attention over the moaning of the souls. I set the journal I was reading down on my table towering with spell books, dirty dishes and the odd empty jar. Once I convince myself to open the door I am presented with an alluring woman. She has long, braided, blonde hair that accents her hard, smoky blue eyes. She is petite and dressed in the radiant clothing of a priestess. Any sense of contentment is immediately overwhelmed by resentment and irritation. My hand that is still on the door twitches a little bit but I clench my teeth and demand myself to keep the door open.

"Well?" she states curtly, shifting her weight to one leg, clearly on edge, "Are you Ratsu of the Towering Wood?"

My instinct is to slam the door. Her matter-of-fact and superior tone only intensifies the desire, but there is something different about her. The way she holds herself conveys power and influence, but not manipulation. This woman's posture and behaviors fascinate me, so instead of simply flinging the door closed, I answer.

"My name is indeed Ratsu, and we are in the Towering Wood. Are we not?" I leer and gesture to the environment outside. The dense trees surrounding my little cottage provide the shelter and security needed for my job of contacting and containing spirits.

"I've heard grand stories of your abilities, Sir-" She hesitates, "May I call you Ratsu?"

I snort. No one tells grand stories of necromancers. We are the monsters that parents warn their children about. We are the abnormalities used by priests to teach the villagers lessons about the devil. We are the creatures people avoid eye contact with. We are outcasts and freaks, pushed to the fringes of community just because we've chosen to be different.

"I am Alyndra of Lerwick, servant in the Church of Iton."

I bow my head a fraction and build a dam around the memories flooding back at the mention of that place. I have trained myself to show no response to things that bring up those memories; my eyes are hard and unforgiving. If you show any sign of weakness in my line of work, you will die.

"I have a job for you, Ratsu, if you will take it," Alyndra fidgets with her cloak nonchalantly.

I should not let her in. A priestess should not have any need for someone like me. Her being here can only bring trouble, but her mysterious eyes and manner of behavior intrigue me. I also need the money so I step aside to allow her entrance into my home.

Her eyes survey the scene inside. The wooden shelves where I keep my collection of souls would not be something a regular member of the clergy would want to be associated with, but Alyndra seems fascinated. The spirits make a show of floating around and compete to be the most luminous to grab the attention of the new, unusual guest.

"Are you going to specify the job or just gawk?" I am suddenly self-conscious of the mess but I shake it off quickly. Everyone thinks I am an animal, why should she believe any different?

Alyndra turns sharply and her eyes are boring into me now. I find myself wishing she were still looking at the shelves. She has taken off her outdoor robe that combats the chill of the season, leaving her shoulders bare. Priests are sponsored by the King, resulting in the finest clothing being in possession of the people sworn to serve the villagers. Alyndra is sporting a fitting, cream colored dress trimmed with gold. The sleeves of her gown have slipped off her shoulders but she makes no movement to correct them.

"Have you heard of the priest named Hezekiah Aldnath?"

I feel my posture turn defensive but do my best not to show it, "I have."

"I need you to get rid of him," she says. She's leaning on the table and I inwardly fight a battle not to ogle at her cleavage.

"You want me to kill a priest? Aren't you like 'Siblings in Iton' or something?" My tone is filled with skeptical mistrust.

Not just any priest either, m- No, stop that. I blink hard, trying to clear my head; I've sworn not to let him rule my life. Let it go.

I glance at Alyndra, she is practically shaking and there is fire in her cold eyes.

"He's a corrupted, lousy excuse of a priest. His good morale is only skin deep. The manipulative bast*** is stealing from the church and-"

I cut her off, furious that she could come in here and expect me to do whatever she asks for her darling church, "I can't just walk into town and murder a priest! Necromancers all over the kingdom are already persecuted! What you're asking me to do would sign our death warrant! I, above all people, should know he's a horrible person but I can't just waltz in and shed his blood! It's despicable!"

I take a moment to regain my composure, and in the time it takes for a leopard to spot his prey and lurch into motion, Alyndra walks gracefully around the table and plants a small kiss at the corner of my mouth. I feel my eyes widen and I gape at her.

"Now who's gawking?" She observes my enhanced emerald eyes with her icy blue orbs.

Her figure is pressed against mine. It feels like a sin to have such fine silk against my wardrobe which is the equivalent of a burlap sack, but neither of us moves away. Her hair is glistening in the light from the lamp on my table. The dank, musty smell from my lodge is overpowering her perfume and I find myself thinking that that is unacceptable. I lower my head so that our foreheads are touching and I gaze deeply into her eyes, not even sure what I'm looking for. Whatever it is, I must have found it because before I even notice, I am kissing her again.

Her hands are tangled in my raven tinged blue locks and mine are around her thin waist (I do not remember moving them there). The priestess' dress is smooth against my calloused hands.

The priestess!

My eyes fly open I take a giant, panicked step backwards. What did I just do? People like me are considered less than human, a varmint in the shape of a person. Priests and priestesses are considered the opposite. They are the closest to being Iton as a human can get. For someone like me to touch someone like her would be weighed as one of the highest penalties against the Kingdom's laws.

"Ratsu?" Alyndra looks at me as if she sees as something greater than a monster, an equal even.

"It's treason to touch a priestess. I'll be hung," I fix her a suspicious glare, "Why are you here? What do you aim to achieve by being here?"

"I've already presented my concerns to you," Alyndra states, ice lining her voice making it shrill, "If you refuse to help me I will leave and never speak of this occurrence to anyone, but I will plead to you once more, get rid of him. The master of the church has fallen ill and he plans to leave his position to Hezekiah. If this truly transpires, our followers will turn away. There is already unrest because of his high position. If he is chosen for our new leader disaster will fall."

I study her. She is clearly here on behalf of her people; her statements have made that obvious. When I search her eyes I see that she genuinely cares about her religion.

An exasperated sigh escapes my lips, "Alright, I'll take the job."

Alyndra steps towards me and opens her mouth, perhaps to thank me, but I hold up my hand and continue, "On a few conditions. I get to choose when and where to do it. Also, you won't be anywhere near me when I decide to act. I don't need you trying to help and inevitably getting in the way."

I would like to limit the death I'm accountable for.

She bows her head in what I assume she thinks is respect, "Of course."

"Good."

With a small nod and a whooshing as her cape flies back on, Alyndra walks off into the woods, in the direction of town, all the spirits bidding her farewell. She does not respond at all, she cannot hear them. I am the only one who can.

***

I lie awake that night, wrestling with the voices that beg for attention across the room.

"You're going to mess it up," Boris, the first soul I ever collected, says.

"Shut up Boris or I swear to Iton, I will throw your jar outside."

"Ooh! Do it! Boris is always poking fun at my essence," Karlin, the shrimpy and most radiant of spirits exclaims from her shelf.

"Oh, no you won't," Boris sighs with a bored sigh, completely ignoring Karlin, "You may as well open the lid and let me dissipate into the atmosphere. What's your plan anyway?"

I rip my pillow out from underneath me and try to block out Boris with it, omitting his question entirely.

"Jean," Karlin whines, "Could you tell Boris to be quiet? He's not listening to me."

"Boris, shut up and go to Hell," Jean states irritably.

Once I harvest a soul, their main and most important memories are transferred into me. This creates a bond with the soul and me right away, but it is not the most mentally safe way of doing so. Before Jean died and I harvested his soul, he had a little sister, Rai. He always hated himself for leaving her in his home with their alcoholic mother. I remember walking back to my cottage, holding Jean's jar as he silently mourned the loss of his sibling, and I mourned with him.

As soon as I brought Karlin home, Jean had deemed her as an adoptive spirit sister and will not hesitate to protect her.

"It's not my fault he's an inexperienced, lazy, good for nothing, freak," Boris states dramatically. I can envision him speaking with his arms waving around, trying to make his point.

"Leave him alone, Boris," Kathleen, the oldest and most rational of the spirits, defends me, "He needs his rest and none of you are making it easier for him."

I roll over to face the musty wall and barely make out my words before surrendering to the sleep that I so desperately need, "Thanks Mum."

I am falling through the air. The wind is screaming in my ears and my mouth is hanging agape in a continuous, silent plea for help. I land in a heap of my lanky, awkward limbs and groan as I push myself into a kneeling stance. I am inside a small house.

The house has minimal decoration and is a cleanly miracle in this day and age of dust and mud everywhere. The smell of cinnamon and honey envelopes around me, making my head spin a bit more than it already is.

A door squeaking open causes me to jump and turn my head to see a strong middle aged man looking right over me into the far corner of the room. He does not notice me in the slightest, but that does nothing to lessen the feeling of panic rising in my throat and the knot in my stomach.

"Kathleen!" the man says in a fierce, fiery voice. My eyes dart to the place the man's words are directed. A tall woman with golden brown hair hanging loosely on her shoulders is sitting on a beat up chair, a book held against her chest.

She relaxes her shoulders, but I notice the struggle in her eyes to do so. I have experienced that struggle so many times before.

"Hello dear," she says sweetly. She deserves some credit for seeming so relaxed and making sure her voice doesn't crack. She stands up carefully and moves towards the small bookshelf beside the chair. The man grabs at Kathleen's arm harshly and snatches the book out of her hand roughly. His sneer when he sees the title of the book twists his face into something fearsome.

"Necromancy?" he hisses at her, his knuckles around her wrist are white, "This is unacceptable behavior! I've spoken to you about this countless times before!"

His saliva glistens on Kathleen's face. She doesn't say anything.

"You are under my roof so you will abide by my rules!"

When he only receives a meek nod in return, his temper flares even more. In a flash, his free hand has raised and come back down onto Kathleen's cheek with enough force to send her to the floor. She pushes herself back up only to be kicked in her stomach.

The man grabs onto Kathleen's hair and squats down to look into his wife's eyes.

"No more blasphemy or rubbish! You are the wife of a priest, act like one!"

His voice leaves no room for any response other than, "Of course dear."

The man throws the book and it hits the wall, resulting in a huge thud causing Kathleen and I to wince in unison.

A knock at the front door grabs the man's attention. He pulls Kathleen up hastily, dusts himself off and scurries over to the front door.

Three men and two women walk in, all wearing priest's clothing. The man beams at his colleagues, all of the anger in his face suddenly gone, "Welcome! Come in. Come in. Kathleen, will you get us some refreshments?"

Kathleen tilts her head so her hair covers the raw skin where her husband had hit her only moments ago.

"Of course. I'll get right on that," she beams as if everything were fine. The door connecting this room to the rest of the house closes swiftly as Kathleen hurries towards the kitchen.

Only a second later, the door opens again and reveals a scrawny gangly boy, about the age of twelve. His raven hair is brushes back perfectly and his swamp green eyes are puffy to match his tear stained cheeks.

He hiccups and turns when he hears his mother call his name.

"Ratsu," Kathleen has her head sticking into the room, "Could you tidy up in here for me and wash your face, darling?" Her voice is tender and loving.

"Yes Mum," little Ratsu says with a small, sad smile.

"Thank you," her voice is tender and loving and barely louder than a whisper, "My beautiful, brave boy."

I watch my younger self walk straight towards the book lying on the floor, it's the only thing in the room that needs to be tidied and study it. The moment he lays his eyes on all the different rituals and spells, he is captivated. I inhale sharply as I hear him whisper to no one, "How is this rubbish?"

I want to answer, but my voice is stuck. I long to tell my younger self that that book is more trouble than it's worth. That his life, our life, would be easier if he just put it back on the shelf and forgot about it. I so desperately wish I could snatch that book away and allow him to lead a normal life.

A sudden wind rips the house away and with it that part of my life. I find myself standing near a lake, with another version of me, seven years older, reading a book. Younger me is with another boy. He is tall and muscular with messy, dishwater blond hair. His shirt is discarded on the ground revealing a chiseled chest. His whole torso is riddled with freckles that accentuate the playful nature in his deep brown eyes.

"Come on Rat!" the boy yelps as he jumps into the crystal clear lake, sending a spray of water toward his companion.

"Iton, Boris! You'll ruin my book!"

"Oh, wah, wah," Boris mocks, "It's not like that book will cure Infernal Delirium. Come on in, the water's fine…"

He drifts off, floating on his back singing in his charmingly rich voice about how nice the water is.

The panic and dread doubles in my gut but I can't turn away as nineteen-year-old-Ratsu voices another concern to no one in particular, "The storm's coming closer."

The serene atmosphere disappears a moment later. A flash of lightning cracks the sky open and the thunder crashes and overwhelms any other noises. I watch the younger version of me jump up from the book of necromantic ceremonies, spilling the jar of peaches he was munching on. Nineteen-year-old-me looks with fear out on the lake and finds what he dreaded; a body with soaked dishwater blond hair floating face down in the water.

I clamp my hands over my ears but I still hear my younger self scream, "Boris!" and watch as I run into the water to retrieve my friend's body. The struggle to bring Boris' still warm body onto is long fought but eventually I watch myself open the book, set the empty peach jar down beside my fallen companion and begin my first harvesting ceremony with tears streaming down my face.

***

I bolt upright in bed and struggle to regain control over my racing breath and shaking body.

"Hey," I hear Boris whisper from the other side of the room, making me wince at the fresh memories swirling in my brain like a blizzard, "You okay?"

"Yeah, I'm fine." I say quickly. I draw in a shaky breath and shake my head, trying to remove the screams still echoing in the back of my head. That dream has haunted me since the day it happened, and I have grown familiar with visiting all my ceremonies in my sleep.

"No, you're not, Rat. Let's go for a walk," Boris' voice, as always, demands compliance, so I crawl out of bed and grab my cloak, Boris' jar, and head outside.

I locate a body nearby and do a simple rising ritual. I open the jar and allow Boris to gain control over the body. We start wandering around aimlessly in silence.

The soul inserted into the corpse overrides the original features (I don't know why. I didn't make necromancy), but it is still a dead body. So the shadow of my best friend is standing beside; his hair is limp and lifeless and his once rich eyes are cloudy and disconcerting, reminding me of how badly I messed up just because I was young and afraid to be alone.

"I didn't actually mean what I said," Boris-in-a-body says, breaking the silence, "You know that, right?"

"Yeah, I do," I sigh, "but you're probably right all the same."

"No way! You're incredibly skilled and you've done it dozens of times before."

I unwillingly roll my eyes. Boris, always exaggerating.

"It's not the ritual I'm worried about; it's the person I'm doing it on. I'm going to have a priest in a jar, nagging at me for the rest of my life." I barely scratch the surface of my unease and pick at a hangnail on my pinky.

"You don't have to collect his soul. You can just let it disappear. You'll be doing everyone a huge favor."

I snort, "Don't tempt me. You know that's not how it works. I mean there's not anyone monitoring me or anything, but I would get in serious hot water if I just let his soul disappear. It would create an imbalance in the different realms."

"I know," Boris says, unusually quiet and after a moment he mumbles, "I don't like that you took this job."

"Neither do I but I need the money."

We drift into silence again.

Boris probably meant for this walk to relax me but all of the memories and thoughts boiling around my head have overflowed to the point that I cannot contain them anymore. It feels like a giant water fall is compressed inside my brain, making a so much noise, it is impossible to ignore it or think of anything else. And when you try, you are just adding another waterfall on top of it. The pressure of everything that has happened finally overwhelms me.

"I'm sorry," I blurt turning away from my friend; my dead friend, I remind myself.

Boris grabs my shoulders, making me wince, and whirls me around to face him. I can't tell if he's angry or confused, "For what?"

"For harvesting your soul that day," I utter, fighting off tears, "I should have let you die graciously, but I was dumb and scared and I didn't want to lose you. But now you're stuck here with me until I die and you never asked for any of this. Iton, I'm senseless."

We have stopped walking now. Boris is staring at me like I just said I was Iton himself.

"You can't possibly blame yourself for that. I'm glad you didn't let me just die that day. I had so much left to do. So what if I'm stuck in a jar half the time? I'm happy to be able to talk with you whenever I want to. I'm not stuck with you, Rat. I chose you. You're my best friend."

"You wanted to be a professor and now I've kept you here, stuck, with that goal unfinished." I counter defiantly, unable to accept solace or to meet my friend's gaze, but Boris doesn't give up and continues to comfort me.

"I also wanted to be queen, to break the walls in society's gender barriers."

I exhale, defeated.

"Ratsu. Ratsu, look at me."

I don't look at him; I can't.

I feel Boris' hands on my cheeks, trying to gently lift my face. I resist him and pull away, squeezing my eyes shut.

"Ratsu." Boris is pleading with me, his voice full of pain. My heart breaks even more, the pieces now ground into dust and the tears slide down my cheeks. I cannot stop hurting the people I care about; I tuck my chin down even more.

His hands become firm and he pulls my face up to look at him. He is still taller than me even though he is the same height as he was when he died and that was six years ago.

"All I need is to be with you. I'm not upset that those things won't happen. I get to stay with you a bit longer. I'm grateful that I'm still here. I'm not stuck."

His last three words are barely a whisper.

My tears are flowing swift and fierce but I make no effort to hide them, "I'm sorry," I say again, like a sorrowful child, unable to accept comfort,

powerless to see out of the misery surrounding me
like a violent forest fire.

Suddenly, my face is pressed into the grimy
material of Boris' body's shirt. He is cooing to me,
under his breath; sweet nothings in a never ending
stream, telling me that it's not my fault, he's not
mad, I'm so brave, I'm okay I'm okay.

It might just be because I am distraught but I
swear, even though it is not his actual body, Boris
still smells like Boris. Like sweet grass and
peppermint. And as long as he is here telling me I
am okay, then perhaps I will be.

I survey the scene in front of me. In the
blackness of night, you cannot tell that this terrain
was once a battlefield. There are many buried
carcasses underneath the seemingly peaceful
ground. I can feel the attraction of my talents to the
departed warriors forgotten in the cold soil. I walk
onto the land of bloodshed and execute a
straightforward raising spell, calling out to a single
fallen warrior.

The veteran's flesh is almost completely rotted
away beneath the armour. He is standing in a
defensive stance and is holding a thin knife, rusty
from the moisture in the ground, ready to lash out
if need be.

Dead people are always testy at first but if you
act as if you know what you are doing, they
usually mellow out.

"Lost warrior," I boom in a fabricated superior voice, "I am Ratsu of the Towering Wood and I demand your cooperation."

The veteran relaxes, his blade now hanging loosely in his skeletal hand.

I speak once more, "Present me with your weapon."

The veteran complies and once I have a grasp on the lethal knife I allow him to sink back into the ground.

***

The sky is clear and I hate it. Days when I do jobs are usually overcast and fitting to the mood of my abilities. It is not important; I just do not like the sun. It might be a necromancer thing, I do not really know. I do not have any necromancer friends.

I am waiting for Priest Hezekiah Aldnath to stop by at the cemetery for his weekly prayer session. The cemetery is located in a clearing deep in the woods; the only place the sun reaches the ground in this dense forest.

It is Sunday, I can hear the church bells ringing (even from this far into the forest), and I am stuck in the sun waiting to finish a job I wish I did not take.

It takes about 36 minutes before I hear footsteps shuffling quickly toward the cemetery and by default, toward me. I scurry silently behind a tree at the edge of the resting place. It provides a fair vantage point and good concealment.

I am clutching the blade I acquired yesterday in my left hand, giving myself a last minute pep talk. With a deep breath, I reach into my satchel and pull out a jar. The moment I open the seal, Karlin slips out and hovers in front of my face. I close my eyes to concentrate on allowing her control of the body of a young girl who died from Infernal Delirium. Karlin claims the body and begins to whimper and act as if she is just a normal girl, lost in the woods. Her platinum blonde hair is brittle in death and her skin is yellow and sagging, but that doesn't matter. A priest will do anything for good publicity, including take care of a dead kid.

Jean was adamant that Karlin should not help me on the job but she was equally as adamant that she should. In the end, Karlin won. Jean made her promise to look away when I actually killed the priest but I am guessing that she will forget.

Hezekiah gradually emerges from his prayers when he hears the faint cries of a child from the other side of the cemetery and, as if mesmerized, walks towards Karlin (and me).

"Why hello there," he says gently, playing the role of the saint he has played for so long, "What's wrong dear?"

He is standing beside Karlin now, with a hand placed on her cold, dead shoulder; it is time to act. I cannot hesitate. As I step up behind Hezekiah, he turns around to peer up at me (I blame my luck but some may say it was the twig I stepped on that warned him of my presence).

It is too late to back down now. I drive the blade into his ribcage, right over where his heart is. His face is lavished in surprise and I pull out the blade, now slick with blood. He falls down awkwardly onto his knees.

I drop the knife to the ground; it is useless to me now. I pull out another jar as realization spreads across Hezekiah's face just as fast as the blood soaking his shirt.

"Son?"

I observe the life leave his eyes and proceed through the ritual and watch as my father's soul fills the jar, just as cold and brittle as his eyes once were.

1ST PLACE POETRY ENTRY
(SEMESTER 1)
IN THE MIDNIGHT GLADE
BY: TATE COOK

In the twilight hour the moonlight shines bright,
It falls upon the glade of midnight.
The wolves howl in their eerie tune,
And the shadows know that their time comes soon.
A flick of candle wick comes bounding bellow,
Three figures now gather inside the glow.
Hooded the figures chant in foreign tongue,
In the forest behind a creeping darkness hung.
The caw of a crow was the only sound to be heard,
A message it gave to its brethren bird.
A message of warning to all that come near,
That a dark, evil presence did linger here.
A presence did gather and a vile pact was made,
Now only those wanting for death enter that
glade.

2ND PLACE POETRY ENTRY
(SEMESTER 1)
LIFE
BY: TASSI JAVORSKY

We both were born.
We both will die.
What happens in between?
That is ours to decide.

3RD PLACE POETRY ENTRY
(SEMESTER 1)
ON HALLOWEEN
BY: LACEY BRYDEN-REID

On Halloween,
The clowns are purging,
The Ghouls are scaring,
The horror movies are playing,
On Halloween,
The children dress up,
The people lock up,
The community lights up,
On Halloween,
The wolves all howl,
The cats all scowl,
And the bats are fowl,
On Halloween,
The dead come back to life.

1ST PLACE SHORT STORY (SEMESTER 2)
SYMBOL OF PAIN, MONSTER WITHIN
BY: JOSIE KJEMHUS

Mason reluctantly opens his eyes to find the familiar monster step through his door into his bedroom. He feels the urge to scream for help, but knows from past experience that it never does any good. The black figure casts a supernatural shadow that exaggerates the suspense and fright, paralyzing Mason under the covers. As the creature approaches, the little boy cowers to its power, and prays that it won't last long.

***

Carla Dayes sips on her steaming cup of coffee while her four year old son Mason plays with his cereal. While her husband Daniel is at work selling overpriced sports cars. Carla will spend the majority of her day tending to Mason's needs and wants, often forgetting her own.

Repetitiously, Mason kept clinking his spoon against his bowl, zoned out in his own world. She watches as his almond colored eyes were twitching with tears. Worried, Carla rubs his shoulder. "Buddy, are you feeling alright?"

"No," Mason whispers quietly.

"What's wrong?" Carla puts her hand on his tender forehead.

"Mommy, the monster was in my room again last night," he rests his head on the dinner table.

His mother's soft hands caress his fragile shoulders, "Mason, I'm sure it was just the trees casting a shadow on your wall. What did the monster look like this time?"

"The monster is as tall as Daddy, and as black as those pillows. I can never see its face, except glowing red eyes… But when the skin peels off there is always a big black marking on its chest with a bunch of curly lines."

"I will check out every inch of your room before bed tonight. I promise that the monster won't hurt you. It's just in your imagination. We should slow down with all of those TV shows, maybe you're having nightmares from them, okay?" Carla embraces her son warmly.

"Okay Mommy. What if the monster hurts me?"

"I would not let anything happen to you, Mason. Go on and brush your teeth please."

***

Mason is laying on the floor in his grandma's living room. The black crayon swiftly moves while drawing in his notebook. The cramped room was filled with relatives celebrating the birthday of

Mason's only grandmother. Carla sits beside him watching her son create intricate cartoon art.

As she watched the image come to life, Daniel walks over and stands behind Carla. Quickly, Carla realized her son was drawing the monster he has been talking about. The figure is all black, with a hood over its dark face. The eyes had threatening red Xs through them, and long daggers for fingers, unmistakably meant for damage. Mason starts to draw the marking on the chest when Daniel suddenly rips the notebook away, tearing pages.

"Daniel! What was that for?" Carla spits at him.

"Mason shouldn't be drawing things that are so depressing! It's probably a sign of early stages of mental illness, or whatever." Daniel turns around to leave, but Carla grabs his wrist. The relatives in the room are now silent.

"You have been too busy selling your stupid cars to realize that your son has been having nightmares about this monster! If he needs to express himself, then he should be able to. Oh, and Daniel, talking about your feelings is not a sign of mental illness." Mason glances up at his mother, and swears he sees fire in her eyes. Tears start to burn in his own.

"I think it's time to go home, Carla."

Mason clutches to his mother's leg, "Mom, I don't want to go home."

"Your father is right. It's getting late," Carla snatches Mason's notebook back, "You can color at home, okay?"

***

The tree bombards Mason's bedroom wall as the vigorous wind whistles and the lightning lights up the sky. Mason lays down staring at the ceiling, waiting. In the back of his mind he knew the monster would return.

Like clockwork, at three in the morning, the bedroom door creaked open as if it was screaming for help. Mason had an unshakable feeling that this night would be different. Immediately, he notices the figure's skin, already peeled off, revealing the horrifying pattern of curved lines on its chest, the symbol of pain.

The figure grows to full length as it reaches Mason. He felt the powerful urge to yell, run away, knowing he was no match against the long claws. Piercing cold hands smothers his mouth, surrendering as he feels himself fading...

***

Carla slowly opens Mason's door to find him lying awake. "Good morning, buddy. Do you want some waffles for breakfast?" she sits on his bed beside him. Mason shakes his head and rolls over cowardly to face the wall. "Are you still mad at me about leaving Grandma's last night?" Mason shakes his head and grabs his neck.

"Is your throat sore? You must have caught a cold from the party. I'll go get you some cough medicine." This time, Mason violently shakes his head. "I don't understand, can you tell me please?" With embarrassment, Mason bows his head, shaking 'no'.

"You can't tell me Mason? You can't speak?"

***

"I am telling you, Daniel. Mason can't speak. No- I am his mother. I know when he is playing games with me. I'm at the doctor's office right now- what do you mean go home? There is something wrong with our son!" Carla ends the phone call with anger in the empty waiting room.

"Mason Dayes, room three please." the nurse calls monotonically. Immediately, Carla picks Mason up and jogs to the doctor's office. Waiting for them is Doctor Sandovan.

"Good morning Mason and Mrs. Dayes. What seems to be the problem with this young fella?" The doctor's grey hair falls to one side of his face, his half-moon glasses sitting on his nose, peering down at Mason.

Carla chokes on her emotions, "My son can't talk. He's been feeling fine all week, hasn't had a fever or anything. He never complained of a sore throat, then he woke up today unable to speak," a silent pause, "Doctor, I know when Mason is playing tricks on me. As well as I know when he's scared, and the look he gives me shows me that he's trying and fails." Carla's eyes bleed with fear.

"I'm sorry to hear this, Mrs. Dayes. I'm going to have to run some tests to rule out physical damage to the vocal cords, but in the case that the results rule out anything physical, we will determine if it's psychological. Often with children going mute, it is a temporary coping mechanism that stems from an anxiety disorder."

***

"The tests ruled out physical damage as the cause of Mason's muteness. At this point, our next step is to narrow down the psychological cause, diagnose and try to create a treatment plan," Dr. Sandovan opens his client folder and pulls his glasses down to his nose. Mason sits on Carla's lap, paying no attention to the doctor's theories.

"How do you diagnose a mental concern?"

"In Mason's case I can only ask him a series of yes and no questions, until I eliminate all the possibilities I can. Have you noticed a change in your son's emotional state? For example, excessive crying or mood swings?"

"He's been a happy kid, and more expressive lately…"

"Interesting, how has he been sleeping? Any changes in his sleeping pattern?"

"Oh..." realization kicked in.

"Can you tell me about it Mrs. Dayes?"

"He has been complaining about nightmares. Mason describes a black figure with a certain marking on his chest. Am I a bad mother? I told him it's his imagination. Did it affect him this severely?" Carla begins to cry.

"Ma'am, it's not your fault. Imagination may be the case. Do you mind if I ask Mason a few questions?"

"Of course not," Carla instructs Mason to stand up and sit on the purple chair in front of the doctor.

"Mason, can I ask you a few questions? If you are uncomfortable, we can stop. You only have to nod yes or no, understood?" Mason nods his head yes.

"Do you know the monster's name that visits you?" Anticipation suffocated Carla with aggressive hands. Mason stares at the doctor for a moment before he shakes his head no.

"Does this monster visit you at nighttime while you are sleeping?" An uncertain nod comes from Mason.

"Is there ever more than one monster?" Mason is getting frustrated and makes his no obvious.

"Does this monster scare you?" Dr. Sandovan presses on, once Mason confirms.

"Does this monster hurt you?" Mason nods his head violently.

Dr. Sandovan slowly sets his folder down, puts his glasses on his desk and stares at the floor. He begins to speak slowly, "Elective Mutism is a form of an anxiety disorder, in which a person capable of speech, cannot speak at all. They often stay silent regardless of possible consequences like embarrassment or punishment. The cause of this disorder can be difficult to pinpoint. Psychologists often attribute the disorder to a coping mechanism due to a traumatic event."

Carla interjects, "Traumatic event? Nothing has happened to us."

"In Mason's case, I believe his Elective Mutism is stemming from his severe night terrors."

"How can we fix this and make him speak again?"

"Unfortunately, there is no special fix. Some doctors will prescribe an antidepressant, but that won't resolve the dreams. Possibly, a change in environment when he sleeps and extra support will aid to make Mason more comfortable to speak."

"Can I make him speak with bribery or something?" Carla plays with her sons brown coarse hair.

"Carla, the one thing I can tell you is that you can't pressure him to talk. His condition may regress and delay his recovery. Personally, I would try to get rid of this monster in his head."

***

Daniel frantically searches for a tie he needs for a critical meeting with a client this morning. The coffee mug in his hand slowly starts to burn his palm, and the unsuccessful search for a tie starts to anger him. Mason is laying on the carpet playing *Lego* with his mother. Two days passed since the doctor visit and Carla now sleeps with Mason in the parent's room. The monster's absence is felt throughout the house, as well as anticipation for Mason to speak.

All of a sudden, Daniel steps on a piece of *Lego* which are strewn across the carpet. Coffee splashes all over his father's white shirt, and immediately Mason is getting yelled at. Daniel rips off his coffee stained dress shirt with outrage, revealing the black marking, the symbol of pain.

Carla watches as Mason's eyes lock on her husband's chest, screaming fear. Thoughts swarm her head in denial and the breath escapes from her lungs. As Daniel races out the door with a different dress shirt, Carla bolts to her son's bedroom.

Mason follows her, only to see his clothes ripping out of the closet into a suitcase, his mother shoving all of his belongings as she can.

With determination, Carla finds Mason's notebook and flips to the illustration of the monster he drew at the birthday party. The truth hits her like a brick wall when she sees the monster's chest; the beginning of the tattoo Mason was drawing before Daniel had ripped the book away.

The sensation of being watched causes Carla to spin around. Mason is standing in the doorway, with confusion in his eyes.

"Mason, I know you are scared. It's time to leave to Grandma's okay?"

The almond colored eyes read *Why Mommy*?

"Mason, I saw the monster too."

2ND PLACE SHORT STORY (SEMESTER 2)
PROMISES UNDER UMBRELLAS
BY: TASSI JAVORSKY

Raindrops dripped through the cracks in the roof. The abandoned warehouse echoed with each drop. A young girl cowered in the corner. A small fire in front of her was the only light in the darkness that consumed the rest of the only home she knew. Her dirty sweater and jeans didn't help keep out the cold. She held her hands close to the fire for warmth. Her long, messy, un-brushed, fiery red hair hid her face. Thunder roared, causing her to flinch. Tears rolled down her pale cheeks. She pulled her knees to her face and laid her cheek on them. Footsteps echoed in the darkness. Fear gripped her heart for a split second. She glanced up to see a boy about double her own age. A sigh of relief escaped her mouth. His bright green eyes glowed in the light of the fire. His only clothing, a filthy black hoodie and ripped jeans, were baggy on his thin figure.

"Any luck?" she whispered. The boy sat beside her and sighed. That give her his answer. No food again tonight. Her stomach growled, making her curl up tighter in to her ball. Two hands wrapped around her and held her closely. Tears began to flow more freely as she rubbed her face into his hoodie. "Are we ever going to eat Zack?" She sobbed. Zack rubbed her back, trying his best to help her calm down.

"Don't worry yourself Nina." He spoke softly, laying his head on hers. "I'm going back out in just a few minutes. I'll find us something to eat." His eyes locked on the fire. Slowly he smiled, "You're getting better at making fires." She nodded. He smiled into her hair. Hair that smelled of smoke and wood. "I gotta go. I'll be back with food soon, I promise." With that he kissed her forehead. It took him a few seconds to get back on his feet.

Just as he turned away, a hand grabbed his sleeve. Zack turned to see Nina looking up at him with big blue eyes. "Pinky promise?" She said as she let go of his sleeve and held up a raised pinky finger.

Slowly Zack chuckled and shook pinkies with her. "Pinky promise." He give her a nod and run out of the warehouse, leaving her alone.

The streets were busy with people walking back and forth in crowds. Cars honked as the traffic got more and more interlocked. The air was muggy and smelled of gasoline and garbage. Rain poured on Zack as he raced from one alley to the next. His deep red hair was sticking to his face and he was miserable. Which wasn't a new feeling to him.

Slowly he scanned the crowd, looking for anyone carrying bags of food. His eyes locked on to a woman with three large bags in her one hand and an umbrella in the other. Slowly, Zack moved through the crowd. No one seemed to notice the boy pushing his way through the mass of bodies. When he reached his target, he bumped into her, causing her to loose balance for a spilt second. In that moment, Zack grabbed a bag away from her, and quickly retreated into a nearby alley. He held back a laugh as he heard the woman start shouting. His victory was short lived when he peeked into the black bag.

Shampoo, a bar of soap, a pink hair brush and something he didn't quite understand sat in front of his eyes. He released a sigh at the lack of food. However he wasn't completely disappointed. It was hard to remember the last time he had a bath. All he knew was that he had gone nose blind to the odor he produced. He gripped the bag and ran around the back alleys. The place stank worse than the roads, even if there were far less cars and people. Garbage, human waste, and god knows what else clogged his nostrils. The roads where muddy in the rain. He was almost happy that his shoes were too small. It kept them from getting stuck in the muck. It took him a bit, but thanks to the lightning that sometimes cracked across the sky, he found his destination. A metal box turned upside down, with a large green rock holding it down. Zack removed the rock and placed the bag inside the box, then moved everything back to the way it was before.

He returned to his alley and watched more people rush by. None noticed the starving boy standing alone. They were all used to the sight of poverty in this city, no one thought twice about them. A part of Zack hated them, hated them all. They saw a poor boy, felt sad, then forget about it and went on with their day. He and Nina didn't matter to any of them. The feeling was mutual.

A voice snapped him out of his dark thoughts. "You look cold," A sweet voice said next to him. He glanced to his left. Standing there holding a white rose shaped umbrella, was a girl. In the abyss of his anger, he hadn't seen her. How that was possible, he didn't know. Even in the darkness of the night she glowed like the sun's twin. A pair of headlight zoomed by, showing him just what she looked like. Her hair was a pale blond and was as curly as a lamb's wool. Her skin was sun kissed, just a bit of a tan, that plus a coat of sky blue, she looked like a human summer day. Green gumboots squeaked with every step she took. A smile formed on her lips, lighting up the alley. "Here," she handed him her umbrella. He waved his hand at her, saying he didn't want it. She frowned at him, her eyebrows knitting together. Her blue eyes looked at the ground sadly.

Zack huffed, he didn't want her stupid umbrella. That's when he noticed the bag in her other hand. It was black, and he could see an apple on the top of it. She looked back at him, glancing at her bag. The bright smile returned to her face. "Hold this." She said as she shoved the handle of the umbrella in his face. Groaning, he grabbed it. Her nose crinkled as she dug through her bag. When her hand come out, she was holding a bag of apples and a chocolate bar. She placed the bar in his pocket and handed him the bag of apples. "Here, these will just go bad at my house. And the last thing I need is more sugar." She smiled at him once more, then ran off, squeaking all the way out of the alley. Zack stood alone in the alleyway, confused, holding a bag of apples and an umbrella. He blinked and ran out into the street. She was nowhere in sight.

Zack looked at the softly colored umbrella and sighed. He retrieved his bag of cleaning products and started back to the warehouse. The rain continued to pour as he ran the maze of back alleys. He could hear the waves hit the hard cement. The old ship yard was void of humans, as always. A place for him and Nina. He stepped in to warehouse number ten, also known as home. He scanned the large dark room for any light. In the corner just like before sat Nina, staring into the fire. "Hey," He called. She looked up with hopeful eyes. He gave her a lopsided grin and held up the apples. Her face lit up with a smile as she stood up. Zack wasn't that tall, barely five feet, but Nina was tiny in comparison. In height, she didn't even come up to his shoulder. She was as light as a feather.

"You didn't break your promise!" She laughed as she hugged his chest. He put down his bags and hugged her back.

Zack placed a tanned hand on her hair and patted her head. "I would never break a pinky promise! You know that." He laughed. He backed away from her slowly. He gently closed the girl's umbrella and placed it on the ground. Nina glance at the umbrella but didn't ask any questions. All she wanted was food. Zack leaned down and opened the bag of apples. They were bright red and firm. He handed one to Nina and grabbed one for himself. She bit into the fruit with a loud crunch. Juice dripped down her chin as she grinned. "How is it?" Zack asked.

"Iiitss swo good!" She answered, mouth full.

Zack smiled and waved a finger at her. "Now, now, Don't talk with your mouth full." She nodded, and took another bite. He laughed and took a bite himself. Sweetness filled his mouth. Nina was right, it was the best apple he had ever tasted. He savored each and every bite. Once done he placed a hand on his stomach. He was surprised to feel a rectangle in his pocket. He removed it slowly. He had completely forgotten about the chocolate bar. He saw Nina looking at the other apples with hunger. "Let's save those. Those can feed us for the next few days. If you're still hungry. I have one more thing." Zack said as he waved the bar in front of him. Nina came rushing over.

"Is that…" she began to say.

"Yep." Zack smiled. Slowly he opened the plastic wrapper. Inside were three rows of six chocolate squares. "There were nine apples in the package. And there are eighteen pieces of chocolate. Do you know what that means?" Nina thought about it for a moment then shook her head. "It means that for each apple, we can have two pieces of chocolate." He broke the bar, and handed her two little brown squares. She popped one in her mouth, then made a face of pure bliss. He soon followed suit. When the chocolate melted in his mouth, he couldn't help but smile at its richness.

Nina smiled at Zack and leaned on his chest. She soon fell fast asleep. It took him longer however. He couldn't get that girl off his mind. Her sweet smile and kind eyes. He shook his head, it wasn't like he would ever see her again. Slowly he drifted off to sleep.

The next day was sunny and much warmer. The sky was blue when Nina woke up. She rubbed her eyes and glanced around. Even in the day, the warehouse was dim and it was hard to see everything inside. A loud bang caused her to jump to her feet. "Sorry!" Zack's voice called from a far corner. She looked over, seeing him rolling a rain barrel that had been inside the warehouse. He was shirtless, shoeless and wearing a greasy pair of sweats. She could count his ribs because of how skinny he was. She knew it was the same way with herself.

She walked over to him, still half asleep. "What you doing?" He kicked the cylinder, causing it to roll a few more feet.

"Well I also grabbed some soap and shampoo yesterday, so why not have a bath?" He answered. Nina grew more excited. She really wanted to feel clean again.

"Can I have one too?" She asked, looking at him with puppy dog eyes.

Zack sighed. "Put those away. Of course you can have a bath silly." He patted her head. "If you help me set this up, that is."

She smiled and saluted "What do you need me to do?"

He laughed at her joy and pointed to some blocks of cement. "Make a fire, then call me. I'll help you put the blocks around it. We'll warm up the water with the fire." She nodded and ran to her wood pile. She quickly got the fire started. She built it up to when it had a healthy glow. She called for Zack. The two of them moved the cinderblocks in place. They were hot to the touch due to the sun. Zack placed the barrel on top of the blocks, so it sat just a few inches above the flames. The pair grabbed some buckets, gathering rain from barrels outside the warehouse. Soon, their bath was full. It wasn't very big, only about four feet tall and a foot in diameter. However, Nina fit in quite well. Zack scrubbed her down with the soap, pouring water on her as he washed her messy hair. She complained as he brushed all the knots out of the blazing river.

"Zack! That hurts!" She yelled as he pulled the brush through her hair again.

"Sit still and it well hurt less." He told her. She did her best, but it still hurt. When that was all done, she was rather surprised how light her head felt. "Your turn!" She said pointing to Zack. He nodded.

"But first, let's get some new water." He had a point. The water was an ugly brown color. They tipped it over, causing the water to run all over the floor. They repeated filling the barrel water. It was a bit harder for Zack to get clean, since he didn't fit inside the barrel. Somehow, he still got most of the dirt off himself. He got Nina to pour water on his back by her standing on some of the cinderblocks. He enjoyed splashing her with water, causing her to yell at him.

When he got out, He shook his head like a dog. Water went everywhere. He laughed. "That feels great!" Nina nodded and rubbed her skin. It felt smooth and soft. She liked the feeling. "You want an apple?"

"Yes!" she yelled as she grabbed the bag. "Heads up!" she called, as she threw one at him. He caught it with one hand and took a large bite. She smiled and took a bite of her own apple. She glanced down at herself and let out a huge sigh. Zack raised an eyebrow at her. She looked down at the ground. She answered his silent question. "We can clean our bodies, but are still stuck with yucky clothes."

Zack nodded, and smiled at her. He stepped forward and kissed her forehead. "Let's just be happy for this okay? Besides," He winked at her, "Now you are even more kissable." Nina laughed, trying her best to hide the heat that was now her cheeks. He laughed along with her. They both smiled brighter than they had in a very long time.

"Nina. It's yours." Zack stated. He crossed his arms, wanting to hear no more of Nina's whining. She held their last apple in her hands. Once this was gone, they would be out of food once more.

Zack should have known this would happen, from the time he had brought the food home, four days ago, the pair had eaten like kings. Two apples a day, and four pieces of chocolate. Now they were out of chocolate, and Nina wanted Zack to have the last apple, even if he refused. "You're still growing. You need the apple more than I do." She opened her mouth, but Zack held up a hand silencing her. "Please. Nina I want you to have it." She glanced down, then took a bite out of the apple. Zack sighed. "I'm going out, see if I can find more." He put his hoodie on and began to walk out. "You stay here. You can come tomorrow okay?" She nodded as he waved to her. Not for any real reason, he grabbed the umbrella from beside the wall.

Zack went to his normal targeting ground. The sidewalk was still very busy, and it still smelled, but at least it wasn't raining. He stood there, watching the crowd. He had seen a few people that looked easy to steal from walk by. Just as he chose a target he hear a familiar voice. "Hello again." She said. He had nearly bumped into her. She smiled her sunny smile. She looked just as she had a few days ago, she even had the same blue coat. "You smell cleaner, and look better too." Zack rolled his eyes. The girl look down at his outfit. "Are those the only clothes you have?" She asked. He responded with a shrug, and looking away. "I'll take that as a yes." She looked down at her own outfit, and blushed. "Sorry, I don't have any food for you today." She sighed and leaned against the wall. She was a bit taller than himself. He could only guess she was about his age.

He glanced at her in confusion. He didn't want to say anything, but she really hurt his brain. He had never seen her before a few days earlier, but she acted like they were friends. It was confusing. He glanced down to beside him. Slowly, he tapped her shoulder. She turn to him with her smile, "Yes?" Zack held her umbrella to her. She eyes filled with surprise as she looked at it. "You brought it back?" He nodded and pushed it towards her. She slowly took it, a huge smile on her face. "Thanks, though I wanted you to have it." She pushed it back at him. "What if it rains again? I don't want you to look like a drowned rat again." Again confusion filled his mind. He really didn't understand this girl.

She looked down at her watch with a sad smile. "Sorry. But I have to be going now." She gave him a small wave and ran to the alley entrance. She turned around and give him one more of her sunny smiles. "Bye-bye. For now." With that she disappeared into the mass of bodies. Zack stood there alone, staring into the space she had been. He clutched the umbrella tightly. He wondered when he would see her again.

He had a feeling it would be very soon.

***

"It's loud Zack, I don't like it." Nina said as she hid behind him. It was her first time going out on the streets with him, and so far she didn't like it. "It smells funky too. The water at home smells better than this stuff."

Zack rolled his eyes at her. "You wanted to come remember?" He felt her arms tighten around his waist. "You need to learn how to do this kind of stuff. What if something happens to me? Then you'll have to find food all on your own."

He received a death glace for that comment. "No! Nothing is allowed to happen to you! You're all I have!" Tears began to form in her baby blues. Zack sighed and turned around. He hugged her closely to his chest. Her words were muffled against his hoodie. "I can't lose you too…"

He patted her back and told her gently, "I can't grantee that nothing will happen. But if something does. I promise you that I will fight tooth and nail to get home to you."

Nina looked up at him and sniffed. "Pinky promise?" Zack nodded and shook her tiny finger. She wiped away her tears and give him her small smile. "I'm okay now." Zack smiled at her and walked up to the alley entrance. Nina stared in awe at the sheer amount of people. She looked at their fancy clothes, their shiny shoes, and their cellphones. Things she had never seen before.

"Now we watch, look for people carrying bags of food." Zack told her as he leaned against the wall with his arms crossed. Nina did her best to mimic him. Both pairs of eyes watched the crowd pass. It felt like hours as they watched the buzz of people. Sometimes her eyes wandered around the alley. Garage bags laid on the ground in heaps, stinging her nose. She was used to the smell of water on the shore. The shipyard smelled of salt and bird poop, yeah. But these bags had been soaked in water, then baked by the sun. It was not very pleasant.

Nina blinked her thoughts away, trying her best to stay on task. Her bright blue eyes looked back at the people. Walking up the side of the path, was a tall man. In his left hand, was a big black bag. A loaf of bread sticking out of the top. Nina felt drool fall form in her mouth. She glanced at Zack, who was staring across the street. She looked at the man again. Soon he would past the alley. Glancing once more at Zack, she moved away from him. There she stood, across from him, when Zack looked up. Nina, however didn't notice him. Her eyes were locked on the man. He got closer and closer. When he pasted the entrance, she quickly moved her hand. He didn't notice his loaf being taken away. Nina stared down at the bag within her hands.

Clapping began to echo in the alley. She looked up to see Zack grinning at her, clapping his hands. "Well done!" He said. Nina beamed at him. She held the bag proudly. Jumping into Zack's arms, she laughed. Zack's laughter mixed with her own. "Careful!" He said, setting down the cheerful child. "We didn't want it all squished, right?"

"Right!" She yelled, smiling a toothy grin.

"Come on, we got supper for the next day or two." Zack said, looking at the crowd, "Let's head home."

Nina nodded and began to walk away. "Let's go." She squeaked, holding his hand. However, Zack didn't move with her. She glanced up to him, and tugged is sleeve. "Zack…" His green eyes were locked on to the other side of the street. Nina followed his eye line. Across for them was a girl. Sunny and bright, carrying a big black bag. She smiled at them, Zack's eyes still locked onto her. Her smile disappeared when she looked at Nina, replaced with a nervous blush. "Zack…" Nina repeated, tugging on his sleeve once more.

Blinking, Zack was returned to the real world. He looked down at Nina and smiled, "Sorry, Let's get going." This time it was him leading her.

Nina glanced back at the road, the girl nowhere to be seen, "Who was that?" She asked, looking back at him.

"It doesn't matter." Zack answered not looking at the young girl. "And, to be honest, I don't know." Nina blinked, still confused. But she knew the tone. No need to ask any more questions, because there would be no more answers.

Zack had been right, the loaf lasted them two days. Now three days later, Zack was back in his alley. It was another rainy day, after almost a week and a half of sun. Zack held the umbrella above him. Slowly he looked up at the cream fabric. It kept him dry as he watched the sidewalk. He found it funny. A dark dirty boy holding a cream colored rose. The light was protecting the darkness. He looked back the world outside the dark alley. Cars still drove by quickly, people still passed without giving him a second thought. There were less people today compared to the last time it rained. Which was odd. This was just rain, not thunder or lightning. He watched the people walk by, row by row. He sighed, feeling another hour slip by. The rain grew heavier. The gently pats turning to loud taps.

Zack watched the people go by. Only a few carried bags. Most were on their way home. At least, he thought so. He always come here midday or in the evening. It was the best way to get food. He leaned closer to the wall as more people passed. Many didn't look at him. Most didn't care. Zack sighed, ready to turn back, and make his own way home. Slowly he kicked himself off the wall. His back turned towards the busy street. A part of him pushed for him to stay. Saying that Nina needed food. The other half counted by saying that for the last two weeks they had eaten better than they had in months. Besides, they could live without food for one day. Zack knew he should be with Nina, in case the thunder comes. He hated leaving her last time. He began to walk away from the noise. The loud tapping of footsteps sounded behind him, causing him to stop. He glanced over his shoulder, not surprised by what he saw.

She was breathing heavily. Her chest raised and fell with each deep breath. Blue eyes looked at him, the sunny smile on her lips. A green umbrella sheltered her from the rain.

"I thought I would miss you again." She laughed, still out of breath. Zack raised an eyebrow at her. She held out a large black bag, shaking it at him. "Here, I've been meaning to give this to you." He looked at the bag then looked at her. He reached out a hand, and took the bag from her. It was heavier then it looked. "I wanted to give it to you the last time I saw you. But I didn't know about your little sister."

Zack did not tell the ray of sunshine the truth, that Nina was not his little sister. He loved her like one, yes, but they were not biological siblings. One day he found her hidden in a box. The box he now uses to hide things in the back alley. She was all alone, so Zack took her in. Gave her some real shelter at the ship yard. That was over a year ago.

Zack blinked away the memories and looked inside the bag. A bag of apples, a chocolate bar, and clothes. A lot of clothes. Some looked bigger then him, some looked around Nina's size. Zack looked up at the girl. "Some are my old clothes," she said pointing at the bag. "The ones for you are my cousin's. They might fit you-"

"What do you want?" Zack asked. The girl blinked in surprise. A frown formed on her lips. Those were the first words he had ever spoken to her, and they sounded rather harsh.

"What do you mean?" She asked him.

"You give me food, an umbrella, and now clothes. I don't understand what you want from me." He said. His hands shaking. "People don't just give things away." His voice began to raise, much like her golden eyebrows. "They always want something in return!" It was a yell now, the sound that exited his mouth. The girl looked shocked. Tears began to form in his green eyes, Zack did his best to hide them. He was failing, as she gave him a gentle smile when one rolled down his cheek.

"You know..." She said, taking a step closer to him. "The world isn't as bad as you think."

Zack tried to hold it back, but he started to snicker. A giggle escaped his lips. He burst into a fit of giggles. "The world..." He said, trying to calm down. He took a few deep breaths. "The world..." He repeated, his voice much more serious now. "It's not as good as you think."

She giggled, a sweet, soft sound. Zack felt strange at the sound. "I know." She took a step closer to him.

"So what is it you want?" He asked. He took a step back from her. A strange heat rising in his neck and cheeks.

Her white teeth shined at him with her smile. "How about a friend?" She said. She looked down at that. Her cheeks a tinge of pink. She played with the zipper of her coat.

Zack just blinked at her, confusion clouding his head. This girl really hurt his mind. "I-I don't even know your name."

She rubbed her chin. "Yeah you're right." She blinked and held out her hand. "Okay! I'm Victoria! You can call me Tori!" Tori beamed at him. He gently placed the bag on the ground. Slowly he took her hand.

"Zack." He nodded. He looked her up and down. "How old are you, Tori?"

She beamed at him using her nickname. "I'm twelve." He nodded at their shared age. "It's nice to meet ya, Zack!" giggled Tori. They shook hands as they both nodded.

They held hands a second longer then needed, causing them both to blush. Zack removed his hand and swigged it at her green cover. "Maybe we should trade umbrellas." Her pale eyebrows rose in confusion. Baby blue eyes glanced up, then landed on the boy. "You're far closer to being a rose," He explained. "I'm closer to the thorns." He shook the umbrella, spraying water around the alley walls.

Tori nodded, which turned in to a gently shaking. "I like my green. And it's fine to be thorns. Thorns protect the flower of the fruit." She said gently. She lifted her hand once more. Instead of wanted it to be shaken, the only finger raised her pinky. "Make me a promise."

It was Zack's turn to be confused, but he still locked pinkies with her. "If you're the thorns, then always protect your rose. Always protect the ones you love most."

Zack nodded. "Don't worry. I can keep that promise. But you have to make me one."

"Okay."

"Keep being the white rose amongst the creepers." Zack said, tightening his grip on her finger. She nodded. The hands were dropped. Zack smirked at her. Her blue eyes looked so much like Nina's. So much like his home. He picked up the bag, shook it a bit. "Thank you." He whispered to her. Her grin could have lit the dark alley.

"I have to go." Tori said quietly. She raced forward, planted a small kiss on his cheek. Then disappeared into the crowd of people. Zack stood there in shock, his skin a deep red. If he had a free hand he would have placed it on his cheek. He was still confused about how he felt about the girl. It could've been admiration, envy, maybe even love.

Whatever it was. He honestly couldn't wait to see her again.

3RD PLACE SHORT STORY (SEMESTER 2)
RESILENCE
BY: NEVADA ALDE

Prologue

What do you suppose happens when fire meets ice? Those who are familiar with the most basic of chemical reactions would propose the idea that as they collide they hiss in an attempt to vanquish one another. When in fact, they are created as balance; their very existence designed to enable an equal cancellation. The combination of the two creates a vast and swirling explosion of steam which is then disbursed into the air surrounding it. Many would claim once it has become a part of the oxygen cycle, it disappears forever. This is both fictitious and naïve. The average intelligence measured in a single human being should attribute to the overall knowledge that just because it is not seen, does not inquire it does not merely exist at all. Just as micro-organisms crawl among us undetected, they may have been heard of, but yet, they are never directly seen unless specifically sought out.

I am what I would compare to one of such organisms or particles lost among eyes that do not simply know, care, or feel curiosity to acknowledge my existence. They all assume I have recently met a crisis that matches their own. None know my true intentions;

I blend right into the swarm of them as they speed walk up and down the streets. They do not know me, but I know them. I know their lives are dictated by another, whether that be a time-consuming boss, an over-exaggerating mother, an abusive father, or an impatient teacher. Their problems wash together and send waves of tension and displeasure amongst crowds. Perhaps this is what creates the overall anger that thrives behind their actions. They have nothing to live for, and if they do, they seem to oversee it and take every second for granted.

Living with the identity that I have – which is in fact (technically) no identity at all. I am no longer a part of this world I see around me. I haven't been since I was a young girl. What I live with is nothing these people will ever take part in, therefore their current understanding of what life should truly mean is beyond them. I live with an extremely close bond with death. I am constantly aware that the breath I take in now could very much be the last. This of course, changes how you evaluate each situation and access all problems. These people and their concerns are laughable to me. I will never be able to fathom the reasoning behind the obsession with specific events that will not actually matter in a short duration of time.

Therefore, I evaporate, and similar to steam, I become unknown to the naked eye and untouched by those who cannot relate to me. I strive for what I know to be important: unseen, unheard, and most importantly, unrecognizable.

Chapter 1

His muscles twitch and spasm uncontrollably, He draws in shallow and exasperated breaths. His windpipe begins to collapse in on itself. He stares into the eyes of his killer; the rest of the face shielded by the shadows casted by a hood. He sees nothing but a desolate void; two black orbs containing no remorse for this hideous crime.

"Please…" He hears himself sputter and heave as the liquid once keeping him sustainable blocks out all air passage. It spills from the long and exceedingly narrow – yet deep slice going horizontally across his neck from one side to the other. He can feel the appalling warmth and smell its tangy aroma; a sweet metallic that he once enjoyed leaking from his very own victims. Now that it is happening to him, he cannot help but beg for his miserable and wasteful life.

He hears a laugh come deep from within his killer and registers it as a woman's.

"That cannot be right." He thinks to himself. All of the women he ever preyed on had been defenseless; frail; alone. He cannot help but feel like this is perhaps the ironic karma that has been waiting for him in the dark for years. It is after all disgustingly fitting that it is in fact a woman destined to take his life after years of torturing the ones around him.

His heartbeat begins to slow; an insidious progression. It takes him a moment to clue in to the fact that it is representing his close proximity with death.

Even with the realization that he will perish once the agonizing ticking seconds of anguish ends, he still wonders whether not his killer is beautiful in the way he would imagine her to be. Is she young or old? Muscular? Light or dark eyed?

Is it wrong of him to question these things when he should be paying attention to the numerous images rippling across his vision? The ones providing him with a quick summary of what his life consisted of? Most likely, but a murderer does not want to relive those moments. He knows of his sociopathic practices, which makes the regurgitation of these memories seem dull, and boring compared to this fierce woman in front of him.

"Old habits die hard, hey?" Her voice is softer than he would have initially thought. He figured it would be deeper and leeched with a poisonous tone.

When he does not reply to her accusation of wistful thinking, she shoves her knife into the depths of his stomach.

"I guess they do." She snickers as she moves from his line of vision and positions herself behind him. She grips him in the choke-hold position to keep him from using any last bursts of adrenaline to run. Remaining in possession of dominance, she begins lowering him to the asphalt street.

His vision begins to blur in and out and a high-pitched ringing that jaggedly bounces around the corners of his skull follows close behind. Spots of white speckle the corners of his eyes giving everything of reality an unrealistic blank spot.

He catches a swift movement of black fabric before his eyes give out again. When his visualization returns the figure is standing far too close. He concludes that hallucination must be one of his final stages. However, this does not stop the pulsating ripple of fear that engulfs him as the figure resembles none other than Death itself.

"No, no. Please." He tries to beg for a pardon, but his voice box is ruined and it comes out in incoherent sputters and sounds.

"This must be what hell brings." His last thought before the hallucinated black figure touches him, and his heartbeat becomes a distant memory, losing every ounce of life along with it.

Chapter 2

One last gargle escapes his fading lips; their pink and plump appearance becoming a sickening ashy-grey. My grip remains on his shoulders with my left arm wrapped around the base of his neck as his legs go limp and I am forced to kneel behind him.

My F-S blade is still being held firmly in my right hand, each drop of blood that trickles off the end of the knife a silent reminder of what I have succeeded. I sit there until every ounce of the oozing, sticky and warm liquid pouring from the slit in his neck comes to a victorious halt; long after this man drew his final breath and sang his final pleas. I back away from him, and rest his head slowly to the ground. Calmly and collectively, I stand and pull out my cellphone encased in my inner-jacket pocket.

"Teo," I begin, "It is done." My confirmation is all he needs, I can practically see his smile through the line; he does not have to speak.

Teo hangs up and within minutes the clean-up crew has arrived to take the man's body away and wash away as much as the vile red liquid as they can from the asphalt crevices."

"You do not play nice, no?" His Hispanic accent protruding from his words. Teo chuckles at me as he catches a glimpse of the man's wounds, consisting of three bullet holes to the thigh, shin, and shoulder along with numerous incisions I had made with my blade.

"He was a beggar; it was both irritating and intriguing." My heart skips a beat at the thought of it. Yes, I am a stone-cold killer, and I take pleasure in my assignments. This is something I will never be ashamed of no matter how many say it is wrong,

I am aware it is against the law, thank you. I just really don't care, whoops. It could define me as a 'bad person' or a 'malicious murderer'; however my job is to take the planet's scum off the streets and away from targeted members of the community. This is exactly what I do, so the next time you wonder how that crazy rapist suddenly just dropped off the grid and seemed to fall off the face of the earth, you're welcome.

"We'll get back to headquarters. You'll receive your payment as well as your next assignment." I shoot a glare that could crumble bricks.

"I always get paid at the site, so do you have my money or not?" Teo looks at me as equally as menacing. That would be my cue to shut-the-f***-up.

Time to change the subject.

"Not that I don't ridiculously enjoy a good hunt, but why the increase in assholes all of a sudden?" I ask in reference to the rapid requests for the continuous kill missions I have been sent on lately. "Did it turn into some kind of infectious disease?" My tone is lifted to more of a playful bite; bait I am praying Teo takes. He may be something close to a friend, but he is also my mentor…and pissing him off is the worst thing I could do. I figured this out the hard way, believe me.

"This assignment is bigger. More like a test." I can feel my eyes haze over with pure bliss at the mention of a challenge. I have a feeling Teo knew how well I would respond, he is completely aware that I never pass up a difficult task.

My mind dances with images of every possible scenario. Something big could mean leaving the city and exploring what kind of pricks the other places of the world have to offer. It also means the chance to score a massive cash bonus. Sounds like something I would want desperately to be a part of, which means there have to be others within our group fighting for the same opportunity.

Before I even open my trap to ask Teo about the others, he just smirks and nods.

It'll be a contest then. My lips twist into a vicious sneer; this should be pleasant. *Not for them,* my conscience reminds me, which only makes my sneer turn into a toothy grin. From the corner of my eye I catch Teo looking at me knowingly; he knows he's got me hooked.

***

Jab, jab, punch and duck, roundhouse kick, two hooks and an opposite elbow.

A few of the many steps that have become engraved in my head and I practice every day like it's a religion. These are the basics that used to get me threw my beginning brawls. Now however, I am no longer 14, and in order to leave the city I will have to nearly ditch the simple combinations completely and only use them if my opponent is already weak and worn out. The concept seems strange to me now, but Teo has assured me it is for the better.

"I need you to use the new combos you have been learning. Combine all of them, memorize them, and never stop practicing, not even in your sleep; run them across your mind to keep them fresh in your muscles." I nod at his instruction, remembering to look at the sparing pads strapped to his hands rather than his face; you shift your focus, you lose sight of the movements that are actually going to knock your brain upside down. So, unless you are getting head-butted, you look at the damn pads.

I follow him through one of the main tunnels leading to what is known as the 'Commons' and count how many people I am able to terrify by shooting glares as they pass.

The hallway reeks of sweat and rotting wood; the old support beams that were never taken down are infested with funguses and most likely bugs that have yet to be discovered by scientists. What once was keeping the tunnel from collapsing is now a safe passage for termites to travel safely; like a little mini crosswalk. The cracked and chipped cement floors are stained a rustic color. The fact that it is most likely aged blood does not surprise me in the least. I've been carried through these tunnels bleeding out numerous times, all bullet wounds; all were meant to be fatal.

The individuals who are *supposed* to be keeping this place updated only half assed placed a couple of thin metal supports running right alongside the wooden ones. I remember walking these dank ass halls as a 14 year old kid and being scared shitless that these beams were going to break and the whole f***ing place would fold in on itself. *That* my friends, is how dedicated these people are in keeping a structure alive and running, and of course by this I mean they are utterly useless. They honestly could not be trusted with something as simple as janitor duty (duty, get it? Anyways…); they'd find a way to blow up the toilet with a plunger…trust me.

"¿Estás listo? (Are you ready?)" Teo asks using our shared fluency in the Spanish language as a way to remind me honesty is not a weakness with him.

I take deep breath and gradually exhale.

"Sí…pienso así (Yes…I think so)."

"Yo creo en ti (I believe in you)." I laugh at him and punch his shoulder. His eyes twitch ever so slightly; the only hint he ever gives of pain.

"Que casi sonaba amistoso (That almost sounded friendly)," I say to him lightly with a wink. He smiles and shakes his head.

Unlike Teo, I was actually born and raised in Canada rather than the dead centre of Mexico. Spanish was something I had to learn in order to communicate with Teo when he had first begun to mentor me. I remember I was trying to pick-pocket the tourists wandering Mexico to avoid having to go back to any kind of orphanage or foster home. I was a determined child…no doubt about that. I had gotten to Mexico on my own; earning little bits of cash here and there, sneaking through borders and avoiding officers at all costs. I'm not entirely sure what my attraction to Mexico was. Although I feel like it was the fact that it served as a reminder of when things between my family and I were functioning. We had taken a trip to Mexico together when I was around 7; this was just before things went entirely south. I barely even remember the trip, only the emotions. It was the last time I remember feeling truly happy. It's such a rare emotion these days; I gave up on it a long time ago.

Truth be told, I am actually quite riveted by these new combinations I have been practicing for years now. However, I have yet to use more of the super advanced ones in an actual fight here at headquarters. This is mostly due to the fact that newbies – or new to certain moves – are prone for screw up. This equals humiliation and a loss of evident invincibility for someone with my reputation. No, this is not some stupid, f***ked up high school cliché with intense desperation to remain the 'most popular girl in my grade'. I'm talking about being beaten senseless, or becoming a victim of murder if the others are able to detect and seek out any weaknesses they can use to take you down to gain your title in the League. We are not all friends here, in fact, none of us are. We are all here for two official reasons; money, and a decent place to stay that is off the radar and away from wandering Po's (police). We fight for our keep, and if you are incapable of keeping what you have, you'd be safer throwing yourself into a dank jail cell.

The League is the basic term for the entire population of people we have living in headquarters. We are – as you already know – underground, and have many different bases across the world that are used as a safe-house for those on travelling missions – which is of course, what I will be competing for. The other bases have different names, or different code words that they refer to themselves as. If you don't know them, and they don't know you, you'll be shot before you reach the entrance. In order to venture out on travelling missions, you must gain a name in the system. I would never have been asked to compete if word of my success hadn't travelled far enough for them to know who I am and what I can do.

I may have an unfair advantage. The fact that my mentor is Teo has given me a much more promising chance at becoming a recognized member of the League. He is this sector's most successful – and not to mention scariest – member. This makes him the most respected. No one ever messes with Teo. Without him, I wouldn't have survived my first day. At 14, I was the youngest to join a League as punishing as this one. If I had kept my prior fears the older members would've eaten me alive.

"Alright," Teo begins, "This is it. I cannot follow you any further; you know where the arena change rooms are." I give him a sincere nod and turn towards the direction of the arena's entrance – which consists of a creaky and splitting slab of wood placed there so the newbies don't come snooping unless escorted by their mentor.

I push aside the wood to reveal the most updated and modern-looking facility within headquarters; the arena. This has always been my favorite space, in fact when I was first brought here, my enthusiasm encouraged Teo to happily show me around. He told me I was welcome at any time, which was a blessing during my first years and has continued to be ever since. Being able to come here even at the strangest of hours just to train is what has kept me sane (or somewhat, I suppose my lifestyle to the average person is in fact insane). I will absolutely never deny my one passion for an intense workout. You know, one that leaves your knuckles rubbed raw, muscles aching and clothes drenched in sweat?

My type of paradise.

A fierce hush falls over the room as the shifting wood announces my presence. Everyone halts what they are doing as I make my way along the edges of the boxing ring towards the women's change room.

"What the f*** are you all looking at?" I viciously snarl. Grumbles of quick and anxious replies are muttered before they all resume their pervious warm-ups.

It's a good sign honestly, it means my competitors have heard of me, and by the looks of it, are pretty terrified. I smile to myself with my back turned to them as I enter the change room.

Chapter 3

The arena is set up to clearly distinguish the separate stages we are to complete in order to move forward to the final round in this endurance test. This isn't some dinky test that you can search online where a bunch of weird gadgets pop up telling you how to properly test strength. The meaning of endurance is the ability to bear pain, and that is exactly what our test consists of.

The first stage takes you into a digitally enhanced cubical where projections of armed men and women are cast. They will either hold a gun or some form of a blade. The gun holders must be killed the instant they are projected (for obvious reasons). The knife holders are programmed to run straight at you, giving you a few seconds to terminate them. They are able to determine your exact location because of the weighted pads all over the cubical floor. Everywhere you shift; your weight is being constantly detected, sending a signal into a computer base that is in control of the projections along with numerous other functions. There are three rounds to this stage, as each round is concluded, the number of projections to kill increases.

Each competitor is given three knives (which they are responsible for retrieving once thrown). They are also given brass knuckles and a suit that are all constructed to hold the same data used in the computer base in order for each attack to register. There are many ridiculously complicated technical terms that are far too difficult to remember, much less pronounce, so that was the simple summarization.

There are a total of 15 competitors, therefore this test will take up the duration of the day and will most likely continue tomorrow. As usual, there are far more men than women, which for some would be intimidating. Not for me however, I like a challenge, and most of the men here will provide one based off of their physique as well as successful assassinations. Nevertheless, the women are just as petrifying as the men; after all, they would have to be in order to earn them a spot in this competition. One of the women I spot on the chin-up bar is known for biting the ears off of each assignment and keeping them in a glass box in her bunk. I'm kind of messed up, but her habit is a whole new level of messed.

I spot this competition's comic relief, they do this every time. They usually pick one of the newbies that has been acting out or openly threatening the small group that owns this joint. It isn't something the League takes lightly; therefore this will be one hell of a lesson.

If I had a properly arranged set of emotions, I would almost feel bad for the little red-haired boy. He is standing in the back corner observing the competitors as they warm up. His arms are folded across his chest and he wears a frown deep enough to make his eyebrows look united. His overall posture is one of complete disgust, and I truthfully cannot wait to see how this one does in the ring...that is if he makes it that far.

The ring is the third stage – after both the cubical and the shooting range is completed. You are first paired with someone from your weight class and you brawl until the other loses the ability to stand without fainting. This is usually when most of the competitors are eliminated. Typically, there are only five in total that are booted from the first two stages.

Then, the remaining competitors are to wait for the entire arena to be reshaped into what is called the 'Battlefield'. Think of it as an indoor paintball course, only here, you're given the chance to collect any weapon of your choice to use to defend yourself. There is a wide variety of weapons placed all throughout the Battlefield, and if you're able to retrieve it before someone else attacks you, that eliminates the low success rate simple fist fighting brings.

People have died during this final stage. In fact, on average, there are at least two every time one of these competitions is hosted. There are always a couple competitors that become too thirsty for power. They lose sight on what they were initially in the arena for. Usually if one becomes held at the fatal end of a knife or a gun, and your attacker is aware, this would be the kill strike. They call out "Death!" and the loser is escorted out. Though, like I said, the attackers can become too excited and actually end up impaling them or blowing their brains sky-high. It's kind of enthralling actually.

"Alright, this competition is set to begin in two minutes! Everyone approach the stage-one cubical and make a *single-file* line!" A vulgar voice echoes around the room as each speaker connected to the intercom sparks to life, some of them coughing out dust from months of remaining unused.

Everyone shifts towards the cubical as the intercom switches on once again, "This will proceed in alphabetical order." The list of names from start to finish begins, and once they come to a halt, I am sort of relieved to be the last one in line. This gives me a chance to know exactly what I'm up against. It's like cheating but not at the same time.

First in line, Edgar Allas, shoots a nervous look down the line and for a brief and uncomfortable moment our eyes meet. I force myself to look away from his emotion filled eyes. I have seen it all too many times; it is the look of pure fear.

This boy thinks he is going to die today.

It is kind of sad to admit that he is probably right. The other competitors will eat off of his fear, and I know this because if I am given him as an opponent, I will not hesitate to use it against him. I doubt I would go as far as killing him for a competition, I don't allow myself to sink quite *that* low. Still, there are others that will, and will do so without remorse.

Edgar finishes with decent results; they will mostly likely get him through the rest of this round. He doesn't look quite as terrified anymore, must have been nervous jitters. I used to feel that way before hunts.

The rest of the first round goes fairly quickly, and before long, I am next in line and am being asked to suit up.

I slip on the wired suit and tie a belt with attached sheaths around my waist for each knife. I push the brass knuckles to their appropriate spot to boost the power behind my small hands. I nod at the man in control of the panel doors; I believe his name is something ridiculously original like Bob or Tim. I would apologize to all those out there with those names...but I don't care, my bad. Hold back your sensitivities for mommy!

As I step onto the beginning platform, I can feel the others watching me with envious, yet wistful eyes.

1ST PLACE POETRY ENTRY (SEMESTER 2)
NEVER FORGOTTEN
BY: KENNEDY LANGLOIS

The thing about being hurt,
is that it's a pain that will ache until it's eased.
But pain is a force that is never forgotten unlike
happiness.
Pain lingers.
It claws at the heart, the lungs,
constricting breaths that only want
to appease the ache for oxygen.
A simple breath.
Happiness, love and contentment are easily
forgotten in the memory of pain.
They are the things that disappear.
They are the foundations that crack
under the force of an earthquake.
They are the walls, meant to protect,
being torn apart by a raging tornado.
The mind remembers what the body forgets.
Because pain is a constant.
Because pain is never forgotten.

2ND PLACE POETRY ENTRY
(SEMESTER 2)
CLOUDS
BY: EMILY MELVILLE

Sometimes I wonder,
Why the clouds-those terribly fluffy clouds
Are so wonderfully free,
While I lay on my prison,
The grassy hill,

I want to be up there,
Free and stressless about
Life and all its horrors
But I am down here
And the clouds are way up in the sky,

I love looking at them in the morning
Before the sun rises from its grave
They're so breathtakingly beautiful
Covered in pink, red, yellow and orange paints,
Floating by like flower petals in the breeze.

They mock my desires,
Waving down at me from their position
Laughing at my dull colours
Of white skin, brown hair and green eyes.
I've never been so envious in my life.

I think about it a lot,
But I am a sentient being
And they are clouds floating across the mesosphere

I have feelings and senses
While all they are simply condensed water.

My dream of being a cloud is hindered,
I'd rather not be high in that azure field,
In the frigid air where my skin would freeze
together.
Nor would I enjoy blanketing the sky,
Hiding the world from the moon or the sun.

I could not do it,
Sacrifice my life for freedom,
And give up the feel of grass against my toes
Or the warmth of the sun on my skin,
Or the colours I observe every day

HONORABLE MENTION SHORT STORY (SEMESTER 2)
RED INK
BY: KISIKAW ROGERS

Psychosis is red ink. It leaves a mark, if you mess up on your words when you are writing the red ink will forever stay on the page. Forever.

Pills are whiteout. The white man's way of dealing with things that we naturally have to battle with every day. You can cover the red ink with white out, and on one side it looks fine, nothing happened. But on the flip side of the paper the red ink is still present.

Cover the ink with some more white out, and it'll look gone. No trace of a thing.

But now you are a suspect, now that the red ink is missing. Everyone wonders where it has went, for it was there one second and gone the next. You would rather not tell where the ink went so you cover up with ugly little lies instead.

You fear that eventually the white out will wear away one day, so you cover the "non-existent" red ink blotch with more wet white out.

Every day you never want people to know your ugly mistake because you want to be seen a certain way, so every day you put on more and more and more and more wet white out on the frail, thin, page.

The soul of a person is a page. So frail, yet so beautiful, so much can be created with a little creativity. So much can be destroyed with a little negativity.

The white out you use on your page everyday makes the red ink look like it went away. It has went away for you layered so much white out on your frail thin page that you made the red ink go away. For now there is a hole in your paper you were writing on, the same place the red ink is now seemingly gone.

The white out got so thick that the frail thin paper could not handle it, and gave way.

Now there is a bigger problem than some red ink on your page. Now this hole in your page is ugly, it is un-aesthetic and gruesome. Truly a shame you had to ruin the paper you write your secrets upon.

You have no one else but yourself to blame this ugly mess on. You did not have to use white out, you could have worked around the red ink. But instead you ruined your paper. Now you can't write down the things that are going on in your head.

It getting harder and harder and harder and more difficult to deal with every day for your made the red ink go away but did it really ever leave?

Where did it go, for matter cannot be created, therefore it cannot be destroyed. You contemplate, where did my red ink go?

So you tell people that you are struggling with the red ink dilemma, but no one will believe you because they want proof. You can swear that it was there, but the hole in your paper says no.
You wanted it to go away so bad, but now you are not so sure about that.

Of course you don't want it back, never in 2 million years. But would people believe your feelings if you still had the red ink present? Maybe people would actually listen to you if you did not use so much white out, maybe things would be better. But instead you are here, stuck writing informal letters trying to reach out to people for help, for that used to work 100 years ago I wonder if it will work now.

Of course, like other things you have previously tried, that idea died. So you say, "My, this isn't going away."

Well, of course it will not go away if you do not do it for yourself. For self-help is truly the only help needed in a dumb, self-created crises such as this.

How can I make these ugly feelings stop, I need them to stop, I want them to stop, I crave for them to stop, I beg dearly for them to stop.

So you stop. You will shut down. Life will be so dull for a while. That is your way of dealing with that ugly red ink problem. People start to notice a change, and they forget your problem and their knowledge of your struggles completely leaves their ignorant brains. For ignorance is bliss, that is why I am writing this. In hope that maybe one day I can help people with their red ink problems, do not use white out for it is not needed.

What you need to deal with a situation such as this is yourself. Self-help is how you will fix your paper, you can never expect people to help you, for expectations will always lead in such a way only to be let down.

So go help your own damn self, you are strong enough. You've made it this far on your page, if you choose to write out your hard work that is your own problem, but that is the easy way. I highly do not suggest it. No one will understand you like you understand yourself.

You're a big kid now, try and help yourself. For loving yourself is the only way to achieve self-help.

Red ink is ugly. But a hole in your paper is worse. Choose wisely how you use your words.

My red ink story is gory. It is something I will move on from, but not forget. For if someone needs help I can look back and do the thing people call "reflect". I will help them, for I have love for them, for I understand them, for they are dealing with the same red ink problem.

SILENT GUILT
A SHORT STORY BY: ALEX BOYLE

Colin weighed the gun in his hand. It was a simple piece of hardware, an old six-shooter that was easy to maintain. It was loaded with five bullets, the last of the ammunition Colin had.

He remembered.

The trees had been green then; the sky blue and the sun bright. Colin couldn't remember what he and Joanne had been doing that day. It could have been any number of things, from foraging for food, medicine and ammunition, to simple wandering. It didn't matter much now. They had stopped in a clearing among the trees, put down their bags. Colin had kept his close. He couldn't remember why. The pair lay down on the short vegetation and soft grass, Colin with his eyes closed contentedly, Joanne staring up at the sky. Why hadn't he kept watch?

"Makes you forget." Joanne had said.

"Hmm?" He should have rolled over, should have opened his eyes and looked into hers.

"How blue the sky is. How beautiful. Almost makes you forget about the End."

"No." He had said, his eyes still lightly shut.

"No?"

"You make me forget."

Joanne laughed and gave him a playful shove. It was cheesy and clichéd but Colin had meant it to be genuine. He and Joanne had been together since long before the End had come. Those years, when he still had a proper home and a circle of friends and a life and an abundance of happiness… Those years were half-forgotten shadows now. Like a language half-learned then abandoned, those times were foreign and alien to him. He could have no home without Joanne, no friends either. It might have been the same had he survived along with anyone else, but something about Joanne had always put him at ease. On some level, she reminded Colin of a world before the disease and raiders and monsters. In some barely-tangible way, she provided him with just enough normality to keep him sane. There were very few normal things left about their lives, but the simple presence of another friendly human being was enough to keep madness at bay.

Madness was something many people succumbed to after the End. Insanity was an easier path than dealing with the real world and what it had become. Probably one of the biggest reasons Colin himself hadn't gone crazy was that he had quickly and easily forgotten life from before. He had lost his standards of comparison. The world was awful now; it had always been awful. He knew this was untrue, as he still had fragments of memories from a time when the outside world had been friendly and safe. Those memories didn't come up very often now - they meant very little. Even the End itself was a vague shadow in his mind, the larger details, the important ones, clear in his mind, but the subtleties lost forever.

Colin remembered a war, but of what countries and over what issues evaded him. There had been bombs and missiles… Nuclear. The word alone made Colin shiver, and he had been fortunate enough to escape their devastation. There had been chemical and biological weapons too, and many were killed by inhuman nerve agents or terrifying diseases. The chemical weapons were as deadly as they were straightforward - any contact with them meant certain, painful, swift deaths. The viruses, however, were volatile things. Perhaps it was the rush of impending war that had rendered them so unstable, or perhaps the ever-present nuclear fallout had changed them. Whatever the root cause had been, there was a single, horrifying effect.

Mutes.

Joanne had come up with the term, a contraction of mutants that was eerily accurate. Mutes were humans that had been infected by a particular strain of corrupted biological weapons. People infected would lose their ability to speak at the same time as their skin would turn a mottled combination of browns. Arms and legs lengthened, fingers and toes became talons. The heads remained largely unchanged, with the exception of a jaw that grew to twice its usual size, packed with teeth to match. The eyes of a Mute were soulless and uncaring, the few facial features left undamaged by their transformation left permanently slack. Mutes were hard things to kill. Nothing short of a sniper rifle could penetrate the thick armor on their torsos, but a headshot from most kind of weapons usually worked. On something that moved as quickly and as quietly as a Mute, however, headshots were no easy feat. They were silent in hunting and in killing, and their mottled skin was perfect camouflage in the forests that were often their homes.

That day in the clearing there had been a single crunch. One small, barely audible crack as a twig snapped.

Colin and Joanne, their ears accustomed to the usual silence of dystopia, had both heard it. As one, they had stood up quietly, reached for their bags as they scanned their surroundings. Why had Colin kept his so close? Why hadn't he warned Joanne to do the same? Her bag was at the edge of the clearing, beside the trees. Colin had his back turned to her, watching the opposite direction while she quietly moved to retrieve her belongings.

There had been a sharp, deafening scream. The sound still echoed in Colin's ears, a sound that terrified him more than anything else in this awful world ever could have. He had turned around, bag still clutched tightly in his arms, to see Joanne hanging face down, six feet up a tree. It took his eyes and his mind a moment to actually see what he was looking at. There had been a mute in the trees, three limbs clinging to a tree trunk, a single talon piercing her ribcage.

Colin had simply frozen up. He stared at her, wide-eyed, as his arms and legs numbed. In his inactivity, Joanne seemed to be infused with a final, desperate energy. She shook and struggled, trying her best to get free. The mute quietly moved an arm from the tree trunk and used it to better hold its quarry. In adjusting its grip, it inadvertently turned Joanne to face Colin. They had locked eyes. She stopped struggling.

Joanne's face was taut, her lips forming a straight line. Her jaw was clenched against the pain. Her entire body seemed to be caught up in agony, everything except for her eyes. They did not express pain or sadness, anger or fear. It was a look Colin couldn't comprehend. He slowly turned his gaze to the Mute, as if to check if it was real. The Mute seemed to focus on Colin then too, it's dead, uncaring gaze seeming to go straight through him.

His feet felt like they were glued to the earth. Colin glanced back at Joanne, at the claws embedded in her side. His mind was blank. Fear overwhelmed his brain, crushing every thought even as it formed. He couldn't think, couldn't plan. Couldn't help. He ran.

He ran far away, as fast as he could, leaving his only remaining friend for dead.

That was the last time he had seen her, dead or alive. Colin had later tried to rationalize his response to the ordeal. Why had he seemed frozen to the spot? It was a natural fear response, he had reasoned, he couldn't help it. Why hadn't he tried to help? His aim with a gun wasn't good enough to hit the mute in the head. He could have missed and hit Joanne. Even if he had rescued her, she would still bleed out and die. He knew he was no doctor. It was only logical, he tried to convince himself, to run away. And yet, no matter how hard he tried to believe this, no matter how often he begged Joanne for forgiveness, he felt guilty. Colin felt like a coward. Someone who had betrayed his one and only friend. Someone who had abandoned his humanity for simple, primitive fear.

Colin let out a long, slow breath. With it, all energy seemed to leave him. The gun still in his hand, he thumbed the hammer experimentally, pulling it back almost all the way before letting it spring home. He was sitting on a short wooden bench on the side of a long abandoned country road. He sat with his back to the road, staring blankly at the bare trees ahead of him. Two months had passed since that day in the clearing, and the weather had begun to change. The sky was now an overcast grey, and the ground was littered with brown and yellow leaves. The air was starting to get cold and the ground was damp. The weather seemed almost to be caught in indecision between summer and winter.

A vision of Joanne's eyes flashed into Colin's mind. What did they mean? Was she disappointed in him? Angry? Those were emotions he would never have associated with her, but were ones that his guilt seemed most fond of presenting him with. Tears began to form in the very corners of his eyes. He took a last look at the gun and closed his eyes, slowly raising it to his temple. There was a noise from somewhere behind Colin, but he barely registered it. He pulled back the hammer.

Two things happened almost instantaneously. Colin pulled the trigger, his hand sweating and his finger trembling, and he was hit from behind with enough force to send him sprawling off the bench onto all fours.

The gun went off, but the bullet missed, and it only managed to deafen Colin. Semi-dazed, and with the wind knocked from his lungs, he struggled upright. He noticed the gun was no longer in his hands, and turned around slowly to look for it. He saw it sitting directly in front of the bench. Also in front of the bench, standing above the gun, was a Mute. It was on all fours, two legs on the seat and two more either side of the weapon. Its jaw was closed, but its lips were too small to fully cover its enormous teeth. Its dead eyes were fully focused on Colin's. Neither form moved, one too scared, the other waiting for its quarry to start running.

The instincts of fear and self-preservation, even in a man as depressed as Colin, are powerful things. Underneath the stress and angst and guilt, hidden away beneath his reasoning and logic, he was still bound like an animal to these most basic of instincts. Such was the reason that, on seeing the mute's claws and teeth, Colin promptly turned and ran.

He left the gun without thinking, instead heading for the cover of the tree line. The Mute took after him in almost the same instant, four limbs scrabbling for purchase on the dead leaves. It was faster than Colin, easily, but once they entered the tightly-packed trees its long legs became a hindrance. Colin glanced back worriedly at the salivating creature. The gun and the moment of darkness were forgotten, replaced now with the adrenaline and the sound of his heart pounding in his chest. The Mute was still far behind, but Colin knew that when he began to tire - which would be soon - the monster would catch up. He scanned the area ahead, but saw only more trees. There was nowhere to hide.

Fifty meters ahead, just to Colin's right, the ground opened up into what looked like a tiny cavern, the kind left by gentle streams that ran just underground. He glanced back quickly, hoping that the Mute was far back enough that it wouldn't see him swerve into the small cave. Doubtful that he could lose the creature, but unable to think of anything else, Colin dived into the hole. He caught his back on the low ceiling and got into an awkward crouching position. He struggled forward. The tunnel was wet, dark, and cramped. A small trickle of water, a dried-up stream, ran along the rock at Colin's feet. He kept his hands on the damp, craggy walls either side to keep himself steady as he hurried deeper in.

The further he went, the narrower the tunnel got, the slower he was forced to go, the more often he scratched and bumped against the rough rock. It was dark now, the light of day only a dim glow so deep into the ground. Suddenly, the tunnel was plunged into darkness. A figure crossed the light, and Colin's blood turned to ice. He froze, the shadow lingered, then moved on. He let out a shallow sigh of relief. He took another carefully measured step forward, but his foot slipped on the wet rock and he tumbled into the shallow water. It splashed loudly around him, the sound echoing and reverberating the whole length of the cave. Colin was still for a moment, not daring to make a single move. A shadow fell across him once more. He heard frantic footsteps from behind.

Colin scrambled to his feet and hurried forwards, all care forgotten. He slipped on moss and scraped his hands on sharp rocks but still he moved as fast as he could, his heart in his throat and pure, unadulterated fear the only thing in his mind. The tunnel was narrow now, so narrow Colin could barely fit. His shoulders soon became too broad, so he was forced to start moving sideways. He was going deeper and deeper into the earth, but seemed to get no further from the mute he could still hear behind.

Colin didn't stop moving until he had no choice but to do so, the tunnel coming abruptly to an end. The rock was cracked, however, and in his desperation Colin managed to wedge himself into the crevice. It was a tight fit, and the only way he could fit was at a diagonal. His feet still protruded into the tunnel, but his head and torso were protected by stone. There was a crack in the rock above him, water and light alike trickling through onto his neck. Colin's view was obscured by an outcrop of rock, but he could still hear the mute splashing in the stream. There was a longer pause between its steps now - it too was struggling to fit. Time seemed to slow as Colin waited for the inevitable. With each shallow, panicked breath, the mute drew closer. Each time his heart *thumped* in his chest there was a matching footstep from his executioner. Soon there was only one step for every two beats, then every three. The mute was larger than Colin, and worming its way in as far as it could go its jaw came short of reaching him. The mute's arms, and their long, sharp claws however...

Colin let out a pained cry as its talons grabbed his exposed feet, claws tearing his shoes and digging into his skin. He renewed his struggle to get away, pulling his arms from his sides and bracing them on the rock above his head. The Mute, satisfied with its hold on Colin, began to pull. Colin felt himself slip slightly and dug his fingers into cracks in the stone. Tears welled up in his eyes as the claws sunk deeper into his skin. He slipped, and more of his leg was exposed to the beast. It grabbed his ankle. Colin's arms were straining, as were his fingers. His back was being stretched. His legs, where the claws dug in, burned with pain. His mind numbed in mortal terror.

Maybe he should just let go. It would be a kind of poetic justice that he suffered the same fate Joanne had. Colin's strength began to leave him. He saw her in his mind, her final expression. His thoughts became jumbled. What had she meant? The question nearly took on more importance than his struggle to survive. Joanne's mouth, like his own, had been clamped shut to hold back a scream. His whole face was contorted in agony, as hers had been. His eyes, however, were filled with tears. Hers... Joanne's eyes hadn't been sad, nor had they been angry. She hadn't been judging him or shaming him for not trying to help. She hadn't been frightened or panicked. Not in those last moments. She had been calm. Calm for him. Joanne had told him, without words, to run. To escape. To live.

The numbness in his brain started to recede, and the fear began to crumble away. His arms were straining, as were his fingers. His back was being stretched. His legs, where the claws dug in, burned with pain. Joanne's eyes appeared before him, and everything seemed to fade away. He regulated his breathing, blinked away his tears. Colin tightened his grip on the rock. He pushed, not just with his arms, or his body, but with everything, physically and mentally. His fingernails buckled and cracked against stone, his fingers and hands were cut and bled. The pressure on his legs grew ever greater but the pain meant nothing now. An inch at first, and then more and more, Colin hauled himself away from the grasp of the Mute. Its grip loosened and he pulled and suddenly he was fully in the crevice, completely out of reach. A quick glance up told him he could fit through the crack in the roof. Would fit.

Colin got his feet steady and pushed at the same time as his arms pulled, and he began to move upwards. The Mute, sensing what he was doing, started to back up out of the cave to meet him at the surface. Colin noticed this without fear or anxiety. He would survive this. He pushed with his feet and pulled with his arms, a slow rhythm that brought him ever closer to freedom. His legs and fingers ached, and his shoulders scratched against the rock, but there was no stopping him now. His hands broke the surface, soon followed by his head and then his shoulders. In one last, monumental push, he escaped the confines of the earth.

Colin stood up straight. He turned around, looking about himself. A few meters from where he stood, the trees gave way to grass. A few meters from there there was a small country road. Along that, another few meters, was a bench. In front of that bench, shining in the mild sunlight, lying on a pile of golden leaves, was Colin's gun. He hobbled the few paces to it, picked it up, wiped it on his wet, bloodstained trousers.

Looking up, he saw the Mute galloping towards him. A voice inside, somewhere deep down, told him to run. Another, more feminine than his own, one he seemed to have known forever, told him not to.

Colin raised his gun in both hands. He pulled back the hammer, released his breath, and slowly squeezed the trigger. There was a bang and the gun bucked, but the Mute didn't flinch, there was no impact. Again, Colin aimed, fired, missed. A third time. A bullet thudded into the Mute's chest. It continued to run. Colin thumbed the hammer once again, and it clicked into place. One last breath. One last bullet. He felt almost serene as he pulled the trigger.

The bullet, travelling at over two hundred meters per second, hit the Mute square on the forehead. Bone shattered, blood sprayed, the beast fell to ground. Its momentum carried it forward, and it rolled in a heap to Colin's feet. He looked at it for a moment. Part of him was shocked. Another part, a part that he could feel growing even as he stared at the body, was barely even surprised. He dragged his eyes from the scene and walked back to the bench, where his bag still lay on the ground. He put the gun inside and put the straps over his arms, stepping out onto the forgotten road.

There was a sign nearby, and it told him there was a town a few kilometers ahead. Colin put one foot in front of the other and began to walk. His feet were bloodied, his legs ached, and he felt as if he could collapse at any moment. But he wasn't dead.

For the first time in far too long, Colin smiled.

CADET WITHOUT COURAGE
A SHORT STORY BY: KARLIE MICKANUIK

How far have I come? When will this stop? Why am I here? Who am I?

The constant thoughts of despair and terror swirl in my pounding head without a sign of stopping. All I can hear are petrifying screams; screams of pain and suffering; regret and sadness. The terrible cries haven't left my ears, they shatter every nerve in my body and the numbness I feel only grows with each and every deadly step.

This barren earth cries for moisture, the light brown tufts of what should be green grass are wilted and lacking. The tall trees that once provided shelter and a sense of protection have almost completely disappeared from my vision. The eerie quiet and the grayest of skies should make me feel afraid. I should be fighting the panic but instead I welcome the despair… it's what I deserve.

My calf burns with every tantalizing step and my gun, a terrible excuse for a crutch, is more work than what it should be. The crusted blood that crowns my face has finally stopped gushing from the laceration placed upon my temple. But everything still hurts. The numbness I feel emotionally cannot stop my physical pain.

My eyes shift across this abandoned land in search for the smallest amount of refuge. What refuge could I possibly find? I am on the enemy's lines, any second and I could be blown to smithereens. Typical, literally nothing could go worse for me at this point. My injured leg begins to cramp and all my optimism seems to be lost… until the fatal screams stop. The vivid shrieks are replaced with a small trickle. A trickle so faint that it is almost inaudible, that slim trickle is associated with water. The essence of life itself. I forget about the searing pain in my leg and the imploding sensation in my head and run. I run as fast as I can and do not stop until the water is inches away from my feet. My body unwillingly falls to the ground and I begin to lap up the water like a dog on a scorching, hot day. I had not even noticed how dry my throat had gotten. It feels like sandpaper. I continue to drink and don't stop until my entire body spasms and I retch all of the water I drank back out in a slimy green matter. I cough and sputter up all the contents that remain in my stomach. Once there is nothing inside my stomach, I continually gag up bile and water until I cannot breathe.

Once my body stop lurching I begin to stare deeply into the water. The dirty grey water filled with silt still manages to reveal the disgrace that is my reflection. I still gaze, mesmerized by my ugly appearance, but all I want to do is look away. The outer exterior of my face is covered in burgundy and the majority of my features are lost in the dirt that is caked on my face. The only asset that is not riddled with filth are my eyes, my pale green eyes. My terrible pale, green eyes which have the tendency to turn grey in sunlight. Those wretched eyes placed in my wretched body. Eyes are the windows to the soul, some people say and I believe it. Only these windows are filled with regret and despair. I want to rip those green beads out of their homes, throw them into the lake and slowly bleed out. If I did not have eyes I would not have to continually look at myself. I might be able to forget all the horrors I have lived through.

I feel hot… I'm burning, I clench my bloody fists and hit the ground beneath me until my knuckles are raw and cracked even more than they already are. I begin to scream uncontrollably and claw at my face, breaking my nails and adding more crimson to my complexion.

Why, why would I do that? Why am I so weak? Why am I such a failure?

Warm, salty tears flow from my eyes onto my cracked and bloody lips. I curl up into a small ball and let the tears flow heavily into the crevices of my clothes. My uniform has turned a shade of ugly crimson more than a patriotic green. It went from neatly pressed and ready for battle to a wet mush of fabric meant for a slob. I am disgusting. My uniform which should be a symbol of hope and freedom has been wasted away on a sick excuse for a soldier like me. A lonely warrior in the middle of nowhere with no one looking. Nobody cares about me at all. Nobody understands me, what I have been through. Nobody is looking for me.

But why was no one looking for me? The answer wants to explode from my disgraceful mouth, it wants to rip apart every muscle in my body, and the damned answer is the reason I'm here. The reason I am here...

It is because I am a traitor, a bloody traitor with no will to live anymore.   A traitor who at the first sight of battle ran away and left their comrades to die. They were my friends, I loved them and I still abandoned them just because I was scared. I am a pathetic excuse for a human.

My sobs grow into howls as the tears flow fast and the memories flood even faster.

There we were, all lined up in identical green, strong shoulders and guns loaded. We were so prepared, we all thought we were invincible. Spent our training years boasting and bonding, happily chatting, we may have been in the military but my squad was keeping me on this Earth. I loved them dearly and I know they all loved me too.

I was so cheerful. They were all I had in this cruel world. We rookies must have been hell to deal with for the higher ups but we did not have a care in the world. We careless young people were only doing what we needed to survive, we did not want to be soldiers but you have to step up in the time of war and we knew that, we respected that.

Then that retched day came about...The guns roared to life and the footsteps grew, our base was under attack. My squad ran swiftly, guided by our commanding officer away from the battle scene. His fake excuse was we were too young to fight them, not even finished training, not capable. He kept mumbling those words as we ran trying to reassure himself he was doing the right thing. He had grown to prize us and I knew he did not want to expose us to the pain of battle just yet. What a fool he was.

We reached the helicopters that would fly us out of the violence, we all made it but at what cost. Our leader dropped us off at the chopper with tears beading in his bright eyes. I matched those tears that day, as he ran back to the bloodshed. He never made it back. I was devastated then, but now I believe he deserved it, one should not develop feelings in the time of war. Serves him right for getting attached to us, attachment always leads to destruction. I, of all people, should know that.

So many people were killed. Some of my friends, even people I never knew the names of perished in that stealthy attack. We were never the same…the jokes slowly began to stop and more silence began to take over, we spent more time training for our missions and constantly watching our backs. The only time we ever smiled was when we received letters from our loved ones and even then it was only for a moment. Our optimism had turned toward dark hopelessness. Our simple job of completing training was beginning to seem less admirable every day. How were we going to fair in the deadly battlefield?

My jump back to reality kick-started my adrenalin. I had to leave this small, out of character pond and continue my pointless journey. This time without my gun. I may be in enemy lines but it is empty and deserted as the Sahara. Even if I was attacked how could I fight back with a busted leg and fading vision? It is completely pointless. It was not even helping my leg I was just holding it to keep reminding me what had happened. The temptation of pointing the loaded gun to my head and pulling the trigger scared me.

I was ready to die wasn't I? I did not want to live, right? But why was I scared? I slowly begin to walk away from the water leaving my weapon of destruction behind. I could feel my sanity slipping with every passing second. Is this how it will end?

My injured leg has not stopped bleeding since the wound was inflicted, it is lessened but the deadly shrapnel is still doing its work. The feeling in my calf disappeared only moments ago without even my noticing. I had to recall the last few moments of excruciating pain from my memory to even remember I was ever injured. Even as these thoughts run through my mind I touch my knee tenderly and no nervous message is sent to my brain to say I'm okay. I cannot feel anything anymore, emotional nor physical; my whole existence will surely slip away soon.

To keep my mind from wandering into the deep pits of depression even more than it already has, I have begun to count. Count my steps, count my breaths and count the puny amount of trees that my wilting body has passed. The sky now no longer a pointless grey but a soft pink as the sun has decided to disappear into the Earth. The terrors of night have found their way towards me. I should have at least expected that daylight would run shallow and darkness would consume the land but I did not, on behalf of a reason I would care not to admit. I had the strongest belief that I would not have survived this long. This should be seen as a great triumph but instead I see it as just another obstacle that will lead to multiple more. Still the threat of darkness and the enemy's main prowess frightens me into the urge of wanting to find shelter. At this moment I regret leaving my weapon.

I begin to hobble as fast as I can through the barren land searching for a sense of refuge for the night. There is almost nothing in front of me but a small look to my left portrays an unpretentious ray of hope. A tiny hill covered in standard sized boulders and jagged rocks stands before me. My survival skills, that are still present in my mind from my military training days, tell me that a cave could be present in the limited hill. The backside of the piddling mountain is lacking in potential but I don't care anymore. What more do I have to lose in this situation? I will surely die from the excessive and unstoppable blood loss that emerges from my thin foreleg before starvation or dehydration ever destroys me.

My speed increases as I turn to the left of the hill in search of the hopeful cave. For once my luck is actually present and a wee opening in the teeny hill beckons for me to disappear into it. Every step I take brings me considerably closer to my refuge, and the closer I draw, the more my heart lifts. Finally, after hours of living in my personal hell something has actually gone right.

The affliction of hours walking on a dying leg and the stress implied with living through the process of going blind makes me almost immediately collapse into the tiny cave and fall into a deep sleep. As darkness consumes me, I regret that I stopped moving. The screams of terror return in dream form and I unwillingly lose control of my mind.

It is the dream that I believed I would have if I ever were to fall asleep again. The moment I left, the moment my life ended. My mind falls into a strange lucid state where my present sight replaces the past. I am standing in the helicopter, I check my gun barrel for what I know to be the 11th time and slowly survey my comrades...again. The same cycle repeats itself for the 12th time but is abruptly interrupted by a firm hand on my shoulder. Startled at first, but almost immediately soothed by knowing who the strong hand belongs to. Probably the only person I trust in this world is standing beside me, staring intently at my face. The words they speak are the same no matter how many times my conscience brain wants to admit.

"We don't have to do this you know. We could run. We could run away together..." whispers my trustworthy comrade.

"This is not what we signed up for. We can escape. I promise that you will be ok..."they continue.

The words keep replaying in my dreaming state more than reality allowed. We were going to be ok, we were going to be happy away from this burning hell. But the world did not like that, this wretched life wanted me to be in pain forever. If there is a god in this land than he is merely toying with my soul. No matter how much I hated it, this stupid dream continues onward....

"Okay let's do it then, I'm serious, we'll run west as soon as we land." I agree with no hesitation and am quite surprised when the human standing near me looks at me flabbergasted. All of the actions that were just conveyed in my dream only make me want to wake up more.

Why did I agree to that? Why did I not just say no? Maybe the outcome would be different?

I just don't know anymore.

The surprised look on our faces only last a moment as we began to devise a plan that should work. We looked over our shoulders every few moments with intense anxiety that someone would hear our treacherous whispers. The trauma we have endured those passing months had changed the way we saw things. What we believed to be heroic acts of good were actually the cause of more pain than the glory we may receive. Nothing is worth watching your friends die all around you. Why did I not understand then that there was no way for this plan to work? With all of my might I try to change the course of this dream to a happier one than what will soon unfold. Maybe if I could make the right choice in this dream it would bestow upon me the belief that this whole life was another dream. I want to yell so loudly that I was wrong to think we had a chance for a life outside of this hurt locker. Why did I not just let myself die a gallant death in the battlefield than the death threat I face with every passing moment.

The dream begins to speed up and my lucid being is swept away from my dream self. I fly above the soaring helicopter into another flying vehicle. I do not have control of what is playing out but somehow the scene continues in a treacherous form. A small glance down to my hand reveals a black leather glove and a bright red button. Voices shouting orders holler all around me and the hand moves closer to the button that will ensue destruction. *Click.* The hand firmly presses the button and the whole carrier shakes. The missile docked away in the inner workings of the jet is released, released right onto my dream self's location. I try to yell for them to maneuver out of the path that the missile is taking but I know it will never work. I have given up trying to change the past and silently watch as the horrors I have lived through frighten me again. The missile picks up speed and slams directly into the tale of the chopper, we spin out of control, were losing altitude, body's fly out.

The nightmare jumps to the wreckage of our transport. I am standing alone, my back is all that I see of myself. My friend's organs, and a crimson river bleeding from the propeller of the machine. I am completely unharmed physically but unable to move my body. My view begins to pan to the front of my person and I will it to stop but ultimately fail. My dearest friends' head is gingerly being held in my arms. Decapitated by the spinning, metal monster. They were saving me. When the missile hit us they protected me and because of that they are gone.

I snap out of my daze to sound of gunshots and large explosions. I am blown back by what I know to be a hand grenade and lose my friends dismembered body in the process. I do not follow code for what I must do in this situation. I am still in shock, another explosion catches my attention, this time closer to me. I do not have time to react before a searing pain attacks my left calf. The outer casing of the grenade has found its way to me. I cry out as the pieces of shrapnel enter my body. I may be in pain but it helped me snap back into reality. I forget about everything that is going on and run. The dream slowly fades as my spirit in the scenes' vision fades.

I do not remember what happened after that.

I do not know how I survived this long.

I awake from the terror, numb but stimulated, terrified but tranquil. I feel so strange, my mind is at ease but my body can tell something is wrong. It does not compute with my brain. It is like they are separate entities of opposite forces telling me two different ideas but I believe both at the same time.

I decide not to get up, I do not even move. What would be the point, the outside world is only filled with hatred and pain. A slow trickle of sunlight from the sky that's outside is my best excuse to continue lying down and wallow in my sorrows.

My dream is still fresh in my mind. I felt everything, from the pounding of my chest to the shrapnel entering my leg. I saw everything, the passing clouds out my window all the way until my instincts took over and I blacked out. I cannot shake the image of my companion's head, lifeless in my arms. The blood dripping from the decapitated neck all over me. I wish that were me. I did not even try to see if anyone was alive. I could hear some of them cry, I could have helped them, I could have fought back. I am a coward.

I feel tears running down my face, I try to wipe them off but only to find I am immobilized completely. Panic consumes me as I try to stand but cannot. I try to move my body but nothing works. How am I just noticing this? The only information that tells me I am alive is the faint heart beat extruding from my chest. I focus on that. With every beat that goes by it takes longer for another to proceed. The only thought running through my head is "I'm dying". It happened so suddenly, I was just dreaming, I was just thinking about my companions and now I am dying. I have been preparing for this moment since my pointless wandering began, I even joked about it. No, no, no, I am not ready, I do not want to die, I want a second chance…I can be better.   I try to yell but my voice is rendered useless, instead streams of tears pour out of my eyes. My heart beat is still decreasing and my perception is becoming hazier and unreadable. I will never know if anyone finds me, I will never know if we win the war, I will never know anything anymore.

I never got married.   I never became a parent. I never got to reach my dreams. I never did anything worthy in my life. I am so stupid. The tears eventually stop flowing. My eyes begin to shut for what I know to be permanent. My understanding lessens to nothing other than darkness… The beating gets slower and slower until it stops completely and all I feel is a blaring pain in my chest cavity.

The last thing I think of before my thoughts leave me forever is how, just how………?

A WITCH'S CONFESSION
A POEM BY: TAYLOR SENEKO

I am a witch,
I am calm and fat,
I do spells to feed my cat,
I stir my potion,
In a circular motion.

My skin is pale,
Just like my cat's tail,
We gather on my broom,
To get back to my room,
We fly so high,
We zoom through the sky.

I am a witch,
On my own,
I trust my broom,
To get me home.

DO NOT WORRY
A POEM BY: TASSI JAVORSKY

Have you ever noticed,
How it is easy to find what is wrong
And harder to find what is right?
Where is light there is darkness.
Sometimes there is more darkness than light.
You should not worry
As the night will not last forever.
The day always comes,
And good always wins in the end.

ROCKS ON WEDNESDAY
A SHORT STORY BY: KISAKAW ROGERS

Wednesday, 2000

This morning I woke up before the sun did, I heard scary noises. It was coming from downstairs, a loud whistling. It almost sounded like a toy I got for my 5th birthday last week... but the toy was on my shelf.

I pulled the blankets over my head and counted to 10, mom always tells me to do that when I am scared. It was hot in my room, but under the covers was much worse.

I got to ten, I held my breath, closed my eyes and ran straight to the light switch on the other side of the room. I guess it was not a good idea to run with my eyes closed because instead of hitting the switch, I hit the wall. I bonked my arm really, really hard. I start to cry because my arm hurts (it is probably broken to pieces) my room is dark and spooky, and there is a scary whistling from the kitchen.

There was heavy footsteps coming to my door... I stopped crying. I cannot move I am so scared. The door opens slowly, and a dark hand comes in, it is most definitely a monster. The hand is touching the wall and hits the switch. It is not a monster, it is dad! I am no longer scared so I go back to crying.

Dad comes and looks at my arm (which is bleeding now that I can see it) he said, "what happened?"

" I ran into the wall by accident. Please don't be mad!"

"I'm not mad buddy. Here this will help."

He held my boo-boo between his fingers and started to squeeze.

"Ow..."

"The blood makes it better Theo, the more blood on the wound the better."

He sat there for a long time making it better. I could see a bruise around the boo-boo now. It must be getting better.

The blood started to dry and it stung. Dad said it will break open if we do not make it a little bigger.

"Really?"

"Yes Theo, the more blood the better. It's like a big band-aid."

He used his pocket knife to poke my boo-boo. It hurt a lot but I knew it was going to make it better so I didn't cry at all.

"There you go! All better..."

***

The whistling was dad's tea kettle, he woke up extra early this morning to go down to the river. I am with him now. We were searching for the best hiding spots in the forest so we could play hide and seek after. We found a hole under a pine tree big enough for a person to lay in. Dad laid in it.

"This is a bad place for hide and seek, see how my leg is sticking out? But we could hide smaller things here," he said to me.

We went to the river to collect rocks. My favorite are the flat ones that you could paint on. Dads favorite are the sharp ones, he likes them so much he hides them so nobody else can see them. It makes me feel special and loved knowing me and him are the only 2 people in the whole world who know about his sharp rocks. It's our secret he said, if anyone else knew about his sharp rocks they might try to steal them away from him. We put them under the tree.

We go down to the river every Wednesday Dad said we won't stop until he gets the perfect rock.

***

Wednesday 2005

Dad said he found the perfect rock last week. It was sharp, long, and light. He hid it in the cave we found by the river. All the hard work we did to find the perfect hiding place for hide and seek finally payed off!

We never played the game yet, it has been 5 years spent looking for the perfect spot. Dad said this spot was perfect because it was dark, big and isolated. It would take anyone a really long time to find a person in that cave. He put his favorite rock there, while all the other ones he found went under the tree. I do not know why he put some under the tree and one in the cave, I asked him once but he said it is not my business.

He invited mom to come play the much anticipated game of hide and seek. Little did she know, me and dad had the best hiding place! I am totally going to win. On our way down to the river dad told me I was the counter and him and mom would hide. I knew exactly where they would be.

"30, READY OR NOT HERE I COME!"

I ran right to the cave. I hid behind a fallen tree to scope the place out first. I slowed my breath and listened closely. I could hear mom and dad talking, dad in his stern voice.

He said to mom, "Stay right where you are and don't move." I wanted to keep them in suspense so I continued to spy on them.

Mom started to slowly back out of the cave, with her hands up. She must know I found them! I'll jump out and scare them in a little bit...

Dad came out of the cave too, following mom. He was holding his perfect rock. NO! Mom knows about our secret rock collection. How could dad do this... the one thing me and him had together is gone now. It is okay if mom knows too I guess, as long as she doesn't tell anybody. I love her so she can know.

"You see what I'm holding? It's my favorite rock. I have looked 5 years for the PERFECT rock to kill you with." I heard dad tell mom. What does he mean? I think he's just trying to be funny.

Mom started to cry, asking him to please stop. I'm starting to get worried now..

He lunges at her with our sharp rock, impaling her chest. Her cries turn to silence. He dropped our rock and ran away as fast as I have ever seen him run. Mom was laying there, in front of the cave. I'm still behind the log. I think she was sleeping. There was lots of blood so she must be getting better, she is just sleeping. I go sit beside her, but I don't want to wake her. I let her be, if she is getting better I don't want to wreck it.

Me and dads rock is beside her, bloody. I pick it up and hold it in my hands. Looking for this rock is the only time dad spent time with me. The only thing we had together. He is gone right now, I don't know if he is coming back. Moms sleeping, so I am all alone. I hug our rock to remind me of dad. I made a promise to him, that I would never let anyone know about his rocks. I am not going to break it. I get up to go place the rock back to the hiding place, but I slip and fall beside mom.

I feel warmth coming out of my mouth. It is blood. The rock went through my chest, just like mom.

There is not much blood coming out and it does not hurt. I need to make the wound bigger if I want to get better. I am tired but I manage to dig a bigger hole in my chest with my finger. I cannot feel a thing, but I can see more blood coming out. The more blood the better. I try to use the rock but I am starting to fall asleep, at least I will be beside mom when we wake up. I am capable of pushing the rock in deeper but that is it. Blood is pooling around me and mom, the more blood the better.

THE LEGEND OF MOUNT FUJI
A SHORT STORY BY: KIEFER ROBERTSON

Many years ago, the god's of Japan were fighting against Aries, the Greek God of war.

Aries wanted Japan for himself. The gods of Japan thought Japan should be shared by everyone.

Aries asked his brother Apollo, God of the Sun to help him find Japan.

Hiruko, the Japanese God of the Hills and Paths made all the hills into a giant mountain. It was so huge it blocked Apollo from seeing Japan. So Aries could not find it and the land was safe for everyone to enjoy.

FALSE BELIEF
A POEM BY: BELLE VETSCH

Under a ladder
Three pennies in front of me
Black cat, on my lap

Umbrella inside
666 painted in red
Warm hands, freezing heart

A five leaf clover
Mirror shards surrounding me
Date: Friday Thirteenth

OCCASIONALLY
A POEM BY: BROOKE FERGUSON

Sometimes
You're left alone
And the only road that you've ever known,
Is ripped out of your life.

Sometimes
When the world seems dark
You become stronger
But if you don't,
Things may never be the same again.

Sometimes
People come in your life
To only help you grow
Then they just go
Without warning,
And you're left feeling lonely.

ON HALLOWS EVE
A HAIKU BY: LAYTON GUISE

The darkness rises
On Hallows Eve, death grows close,
Beware the spirits

Anger brews in them
Their evil thoughts become action
You cannot run, fool.

You can only pray
That they will spare your sad life
Fear rises in all.

MAD OLD HICKORY
A POEM BY: TASSI JAVORSKY

Mad old hickory that lived by the well.
One day he went for water, but then he fell.
He went down, down, down.
And when he hit the bottom he sadly drowned.

Mad old hickory that lived by the well.
He stole the town's southern bell.
He made them sing and cry,
Till they said goodbye.

Mad old hickory that lived by the well.
Took them to a place so no one would hear them
yell.
One day, a little dove snapped.
She pushed him so he was trapped.

Mad old hickory that lived by the well.
When he died he went to hell.
There he laughed, "Don't worry little dove.
Very soon I will be back above."

A SHUT IN'S RELEASE TO SOCIETY

A SHORT STORY BY: SETH SIMMONS

"It's just that I worry about you Andy," Andy's friend Serena exclaimed.

"I know Serena but I'm fine you can come check for yourself," Andy reassured her.

"What do you even do for money?" Serena yelled.

"I play in online tournaments, one would say it's my greatest talent and I've made a very successful career out of it," Andy gave as an answer.

"Ughh! You are so hopeless!" Serena screamed and hung up in fury.

Andy sighed, she seems pretty upset that I'm a shut in, but who could blame her she never gets to see me anymore. Maybe one of these days she could come visit me, he thought to himself.

There is no way I can ever show my face in town ever again, ever since I was convicted as a child predator at that rigged trial. I can't even show my face without getting bombed in terrible remarks. About two years ago Andy was convicted at a rigged trial in his hometown of Tokyo as a child predator and released one year later with probation but now his probation sentence is over.

Andy went to his dresser beside his bed and pulled out some papers. On them was proof that his trial was rigged and he was convicted unfairly. With this evidence he thought to himself, he could probably sue for slander.

"No it's been too long no one would believe me but my friends and family," Andy whispered out loud. He went and sat down at his computer and turned it on. The first article he saw was the anniversary of his trial and disappearance.

Whenever he shopped he made sure it was online and when he did have to go out in public he made sure to hide his face so no one could recognize him.

Andy loaded up Feam, the leading PC gaming platform, and launched World of Overwatchcraft 2. He went to the game's main town and started preparing his items and strategies for this week's tournament. The way the tournament works is that you fight three battles and if you win two you advance to the next tier and there were three tiers.

He saw he was fighting an orc, panda fighter and a winstonhardt. He was a paladin who specialized in holy magic and orcs specialized in death magic so he came to the conclusion that it would be a more difficult fight. Panda fighters did not use any magic and mostly specialized in hand to hand combat. He concluded that it would be an easy fight, and that the winstonhardt, would not be too much of a problem for Andy. Winstonhardt's were hand to hand fighters that could use any magic, but with his holy enchanted shield that wouldn't be too much of a problem.

As expected he won the first tier and fought the same kind of enemies in the next two tiers and won the tournament. Like always Slizzard, the company that made the game, forwarded him the prize money but this time he got a peculiar email as well.

It read, "Congratulations on your winning streak! You have a current winning streak of 250 that enables you to an increased prize of $100,000, and an all-expense paid trip for two to the Phaz South Gaming convention in Dallas, Texas. The convention is next weekend, and we have booked you 2 rooms in the Sarwik Melclose Hotel near the convention center. Start packing and we will have someone deliver the tickets to your house ASAP."

Andy thought to himself, oh my god, two tickets to the Phaz South in Texas. I can actually go there because no one will know who I am there, and I can bring Serena, this is great!

Andy quickly called Serena and told her what happened and she ecstatically agreed to join him. When the weekend rolled around they both met at the airport with their luggage. Andy was in his disguise, when he had to go through security or a baggage check he turned and sneezed or coughed.

"You're a free man now it's not like they'll lock you up or anything." Serena stated in an annoyed tone.

"It's not that I think they'll throw me in jail it's that they will ridicule me and hate me." Andy whispered.

"Whatever." Serena retorted.

After a long 7 hour flight they arrived in Dallas, Texas. They stepped out of the airport, grabbed a taxi and took it to the Sarwik Melclose Hotel.

Andy and Serena unpacked their bags and ordered room service. The food was some American cuisine, salsa and chips, buffalo spicy burgers and whiskey.

"Oh I love chips and salsa!" Serena shouted with excitement in her voice.

"Yeah the food looks good but I don't drink alcohol," Andy whispered shyly.

"Don't be such a pansy!" she exclaimed. Serena was already done her whisky before she even touched her food.

"Boy you really like whiskey don't you" Andy pointed out.

"Yeah it's good, I try not to make it a regular habit."

After they finished their food and drinks they said bye for the night and Serena headed to her own room. Andy tried to sleep but had to many thoughts going through his head.

"What if someone recognizes me here?" he thought to himself. "Hopefully they don't know who I am and kick me out," he whispered. He spent the better part of that night worrying about the next day. Andy only got five hours of sleep that night and he woke up exhausted.

When Serena woke up she went to Andy's room and woke him up. The Convention Center was close enough that they could walk there in five minutes. The event had just started when they got there. Most of the stations were filled to the brim but Andy and Serena ultimately decided to go watch the esport event. When they got there the host was giving the introduction.

"What is up esports nation?   I'm your host Killer Keemstar, and let's get riiiiight into the games!"

Andy thought to himself, 'That's very obnoxious.'

"I'm here today with the HaZe and Sloptic teams who are gonna battle it out in World of Overwatchctraft 2.

After the esports competition was over Serena went to go to the Slizzard booth and Andy was hungry so he went to grab some food.

Andy was at the food court and he got some Brooklynn fried chicken, he was walking to find a table when a girl bumped into him and caused him to drop his food.

"Oh I'm so sorry I wasn't looking where I was going, I'll buy you some new food," The girl expressed guiltily.

"Ok sure, sorry if I act kind of awkward, I am kind of a shut in." Andy whispered.

"Oh why is that?" The girl asked.

"It's a long story," he told her.

"I'm willing to listen to it!" she expressed with great interest.

"Alright here goes: about two years ago I was an employee at a fast food place. A young girl and her parents walked in and handed me a court summons on the grounds of pedophilia. I had never met that girl. When I got to the court I could tell the jury had already made up their mind. The decision was rigged to go against me, long story short, I got one year in prison and one year of probation and had to pay them $6,800 in damages." Andy told her.

"Oh wow, that's unfortunate, but that was two years ago I'm sure people have forgot about it," the girl reassured him.

"No, there's no way I can ever show my face to my town again," Andy told her in disappointment.

"Come on, after we eat I'll take you on a date and show you how fun it is to be a part of society!" she exclaimed in excitement.

"No I don't want to." He told her.

"Come on after this I'll stop bugging you, oh that's right I haven't told you my name yet. It's Akine what's yours?" Akine asked.

"It's Andy and fine I'll go," he replied.

Andy called Serena and told her what he was doing and she told him to meet up with her afterwards.

Akine took him to the EA booth to try talking to random people. Andy approached a guy holding a basketball covering his chin.

"Hi I'm Andy, what's your name?" Andy asked the guy.

"People call me the Leaf man, nice to meet you," the guy answered.

Andy thought to himself, "this guy's weird."

"What do you do for hobbies?" Andy asked.

"I like making videos on kids, surfing in CS GO and most of all, covering my chin because I'm self-conscious of it, " the Leaf man answered.

"Ok…" Andy expressed and walked back to Akine.

"I knew you could do it, come on we got one more stop." Akine told Andy.

They arrived at a competition of MKZ and Akine entered them both in.

"Ok here's the real challenge this is a face to face contest and you two will be sitting next to each other, if you can overcome this, you can overcome your fear of being ridiculed," she explained.

"Ok." Andy replied.

The more Andy played the less his social fear bothered him and when he faced Akine in the last match it was gone. He was playing as the character Hugh Mungus and she was playing as Harambe. After an intense match Andy was named the winner and awarded with a neon keyboard and a t-shirt.

"Awesome, I'm so proud of you!" Akine shouted as she kissed him on his cheek.

Andy was in his room getting a lecture from Serena about not trusting people you do not know. She went on and on about how Akine could be a psychopath and how he should not trust her. But Andy was in love and wanted none of it.

"Look I'm tired and I want to go to sleep, just go to your room and stay out of my business," he suggested in frustration.

"HMPH!" Serena exclaimed in anger and left to her room.

The next day Akine and Andy were joined by a very worried and frustrated Serena, but Akine did not seem to mind. They went to a lot of different booths and eventually made it to an indie developer booth where the Leaf man was standing.

Leaf man had an ice cream cone covering his chin and he was eating it very slowly.

"Hey what's up guys?" he greeted them in a reptilian like tone.

Before they could greet Leaf man the esports announcer came up and started to scream, "Hey why are you slandering me, why are you lying about me, you're taking everything out of context you little emo kid!."

"Uh guys I gotta go," Leaf man told Akine and everyone.

"That was weird," Andy stated.

"Not as weird as this," Akine expressed while she leaned in and stole a kiss from Andy.

Serena lost it and yelled "Get off of him!"

"Why, you two aren't dating are you?" Akine asked.

"No but still you two just met, it's not right," Serena replied.

"I'll ask you not to decide what's right and what's not for us." Akine asked in a sassy voice.

Serena stormed away but not before slapping Akine so hard that she fell to the ground.

For the rest of the day Andy and Akine went to booths and hung out while Serena was at the hotel moping and feeling bad about what she did.

Day two of three of the convention was almost over but Akine had one more surprise for Andy.

She took him to a room with a mother, her daughter and a very angry looking judge.

"What's going on here?" asked Andy.

The judge spoke. "This girl, Akine, has brought to my attention that the outcome of your trial was rigged by the jury. The ruling you were given was due to the actions of these two ladies greed. The jury all had ties to them and they agreed to convict you as long as they got a cut. I apologize for your sentence and I have already got you money for damages, loss of income and loss of enjoyment of life from these two ladies."

"W-wait how did you know Akine wasn't lying!?" Andy asked in shock.

"These two women confessed, I hope you accept their apology and mine," the judge answered respectfully.

"Yes I accept your apologies and thank you for clearing things up," Andy told them.

"Ok we will be off now," the judge stated and walked off with the women.

Before she could say anything Akine had Andy's arms around her and he kept constantly thanking her until she interrupted him with a kiss.

The next day when Andy woke up Serena was already awake in her room pacing around anxiously. Serena walked into Andy's room and apologized for everything.

Andy had already forgiven her so he accepted her apology and they left for the convention center.

Akine was nowhere to be seen and they spent half the day looking for her. They assumed she was sick or had some sort of emergency she had to deal with and did not have time to call or text them.

For the rest of the day Serena and Andy competed in gaming contests and spent time at booths until Andy got a phone call.

"Is this Andy Raradine?" the voice asked. The voice sounded very professional and very serious so Andy replied with a formal yes.

"Hello I'm Akine's doctor, I'm very sorry to have to inform you but late last night the hospital where I work received a call from a hotel in Texas. Akine was found dead in her hotel room," the doctor informed Andy.

Andy was left speechless, he had no words.

The doctor answered, "She had cancer, that was the cause of her death. That's not all she left a note for you and she wanted you to have it, again I'm very sorry."

Andy put his phone away and thoughts rushed through his head. "This has to be a joke, this can't be happening."

Serena asked what the call was about and Andy told her and Serena had the same reaction. They both went back to her hotel where they both sobbed harder than they ever had before.

Andy heard a knock at his door. He opened it and it was a cleaning lady but she was not wearing this hotel's uniform. The lady handed him a note and told him that the instructions told whoever found it to give it to his hotel room.

Andy asked Serena to come to his room and he read the note out loud,

"Dear Andy and Serena, I'm sure you've already heard about my condition and my death. I'm sorry I didn't tell you earlier, but I was afraid if I did you wouldn't associate with me. Andy, I truly did love you.

When I was fifteen both my parents were doctors in Iraq helping soldiers and civilians. They were both heroes, they were killed in action. I wanted to be just like them and help people before I died. When I met you Andy, I loved you and the more I helped you, the more it was less about heroism and more about you. I want to help you one last time, I arranged my funeral to be in your home town and anyone can go. Please come and see me one last time, the address for it is on the back. Love Akine."

Andy was holding the note crying.

Serena asked. "What are you gonna do?"

Andy told her. "I guess the first step to reintegrating to society would be Akine's funeral."

DECISIONS, DECISIONS
A SHORT STORY BY: TATE COOK

On a very ordinary street, in an unassuming town, there lived a very abnormal man. The man lived alone on his ordinary street in his unassuming town, inside a normal little house. With two windows on the front, a small garden to the side and a short driveway, with a tiny little car the man attracted no attention whatsoever. Whilst his life was ever so ordinary and extremely unexciting the man himself was slightly more interesting, for you see the man was cursed.

Every so often the man would be given two choices out of nowhere. The choices could be anything from "do three jumping jacks" to "Massive tornado appears." The peculiar part was, whatever choice the man picked it would always come true. The man was not happy, he had a nice job, and alright house, but the curse was changing all of that. "Why?!" he shouted "Why must you punish me so God?" but nothing happened.

Suddenly a voice boomed "Choose," it exploded, and two new options appeared "Move homes or quit your job." The man was furious now.

"Why in the hell do I have to change my life like this, what did I ever do?" The man pleaded, but there was no answer. Now realizing that the world is indeed cruel and unforgiving the man packed his most important items and prepared to move.

"Choose," came the voice again, shaking the foundations of what was once the man's home. "Go to work or stay home and cry." *Wow never thought of that...,* The man thought to himself, but never spoke aloud for fear of angering some higher very asinine power.

Comfortable in his little cubicle at his dull workplace the man prepared himself for his job, and the inevitable decisions later in the day.

"Choose," commanded the voice "Fire or Something good."

"Who the hell chooses the first option you primordial spack basket?" questioned the man, perhaps slightly louder that is socially acceptable in the workplace. Quieter this time the man told whatever the hell the voice was that he would in fact prefer the second option.

A loud rumbling began to echo through the building, and soon after a construction crew made itself known in a rather rude manner through which they forced out every occupant of the man's boring little workspace. The bemused employees were informed that the building was to be renovated as the new location of **Something Good Burgers**.

"Why?" the man sobbed softly to himself... "Alright!" the man spoke regaining some of his quickly draining composure, "What the hell do you want me to do now?"

"Choose," Laughed the voice, "Strip naked and dance like a monkey or confess your love to the next woman who walks down the street."

Tears welling up in his eyes the man managed a pitiful "Okay" before walking down the street.

After being laughed at by a gorgeous woman with cherry blond hair and eyes blue as the deep sea, the man made his way to the new home he found.

As the man made his way into his bed to rest away the day's surprises, the voice made itself known one last time "Choose!" It echoed through the man's bedroom "Sleep or don't sleep."

"What the hell did you think I was doing you freaking ingrate, practicing my interpretive dance?" The man exploded, clearly weighed down by the burden of the rest of the day. And then the man passed out from shear rage.

The man was awoken bright and early to the familiar sound of "Choose!"

"What the hell is it this time?

"Something Great or Something Interesting."

Oh god what the hell do I do? thought the man clearly not liking the mystery of his options. *Anything can be interesting, I mean a freaking plane could come crashing through my house, that would be pretty interesting. On the other hand, something great could be a trick, like yesterday, and something interesting might turn out to be better than great. Oh god, what the hell do I choose? Too risky.*

"Something great" exclaimed the man unsure and terrified of what's to come.

A pounding knock came from the door. *Just kill me now.* The man opened the door and below his feet stood a large matte black leather briefcase. *Nope* thought the man and immediately closed the door. The man knew well and good that no strings attached didn't really go with his condition, and thus the man preferred to leave the suspicious leather case where it was, as if nothing incredibly strange and most likely dangerous was just dropped off on his front porch.

Later that day another knock came at the door. The man, thoroughly agitated that his extremely early retirement was being interrupted, made his way to the door in a fashion reminiscent to that of an angry monkey who just lost out on his breakfast.

"What do you want!" exclaimed the man as he swung the door open. At the man's feet now stood a second briefcase, along with what appeared to be a very extravagant, very expensive, and probably stolen jeweled necklace. *Nope* thought the man as he closed the door a second time.

Through the day the door was knocked upon five more times, and not once did the curse make itself known, probably content to just watch as the man became more and more frustrated with the state of his life. At one point the "gifts" became so great in number that the man just didn't bother to open the door anymore. Instead, the man wrote a note to whomever left the gifts telling them exactly where they could shove their presents.

"Choose," exploded the voice finally, "Accept the gifts or something extremely bad."

At this point a number of unpleasant things swarmed the man's head, but the man knew fighting with the voice was futile, so instead, opted to silently take the gifts into his home and prepare for the inevitable police force to break down his door.

Night came and went as the man dreamed of what he would do to the prick that cursed him. Finally the man awoke to the soothing sound of "Choose!" shouting, oh so tenderly, in his ear "Something interesting or mystery box."

"You know what, I don't even care anymore," lied the man "let's go with the mystery box because that'll be so much freaking fun!"

Next came the ringing of a doorbell "I don't even have a doorbell!" shouted the man, clearly unaware that the voice didn't give a damn for his petty logic and reason.

This time, when the door opened, a gigantic bright yellow box, with a question mark written in elegant cursive on the front, was sitting in the middle of the man's lawn. Knowing full well how good ignoring the voice went, the man began opening the box. Inside the box was a slightly smaller box with a red velvet lining. Unamused, the man opened the red box only to be greeted with the sight of a green paper box, only about a centimeter smaller in diameter to the previous box. After about half an hour of rainbow boxes and tears the man found himself with a small cardboard box in his hands. Opening inside this final box the man found a hastily drawn map that was more kindergarten art project than map, and a card with a single word, freedom.

Tears of a different sort now filled the man's eyes. *Really? Freedom, like from the curse surely it's screwing with me right? Right?* New found hope now filled the man a spark of determination settled within him.

"Choose," Interrupted the voice sensing the faint glimmer of hope, "Burn up the map or burn down your house." Tears of a third sort fell that day.

One pile of ashes, an auction of stolen goods, and an apartment later the man began his search. Library, occult magic shop, abandoned church it didn't matter for the man was determined and a righteous fury blazed within him. *Freedom* thought the man and that was all he needed to fuel his quest.

The man's determination quickly sputtered when he saw the first destination the voice intended for him to go. Before the man stood a wonderfully pink and extremely feminine women's lingerie store.

"And just what exiting surprises do you plan to put me through here you all powerful crap basket?" the man exclaimed like some lunatic.

"Choose," came the voice, "go inside and buy something or burn the map." After an awkward walk through the store the man found himself in the possession of a random article, picked off the nearest selection before making his way to the register seeming with rage. Finally, after what seemed like an eternity of waiting the man was able to make his purchase and be on his way, however the voice had other plans.

"Choose," the voice laughed, giggling like a schoolgirl whilst the man became increasingly worried, "They're for me or they're for you." Hollow and dead inside the man let out a pitiful "They're for me…" before shambling back home defeated and broken.

During the walk home the man noticed something very strange about his receipt besides the splotches of tears. There was an address written upon, it in a light color nearly indistinguishable from the receipt itself. Stranger yet the man knew the location written on the receipt, it was his old high school now filled with new victims for the year. The man didn't know what terrified him more, going back to his school, what the voice would make him do when he got there, or the fact that he remembered the address by heart.

Once the man reached the school something felt different. He had decided to show up for once so that might be it, or perhaps it was that he had arrived sometime in the afternoon, or maybe, just maybe, it was the small Chihuahua sitting outside the school doors wearing a sombrero and women's underwear, probably the first two. The man approached the dog in a way that can only be described as, I don't give a crap any more fashion, and waited for the voice to show up. It did in a sense, but this time it came from the puny mutt that stood before him. This came as a slight surprise.

"Choose," the Chihuahua proclaimed in a way that annoyed the man slightly more than if the dog had just barked normally.

"Wait, wait, wait!" interrupted the man "What the heck is with the dog?"

"I am the one you call God," said the runty little dog, and the man began pondering whether or not to change religions, "You have wasted away the life

I have given you, content to live in monotony day, after day, it's gotten so out of hand that I decided to do something before your boredom seeps into heaven. Now Choose!" it spoke out interrupting the man's train of thought, "Something bad will happen to the town but you will be free of the curse or go home and keep the curse."

Now the man truly had to think, how far would he go to be rid of the curse, could he possibly sacrifice the wellbeing of others for the goodness of himself, and could he live with the curse for the rest of his life. All this raced through his head as a scantily clad dog ran circles about the man's feet.

This aggravated the man to no end and he added whether or not he could kill a god to the list of things going through his head. Finally the dog stopped and looked up expectantly at the man

"Well?" it questioned "What do you choose?"

The possible pressure was somewhat downsized when these questions came from a dog in a sombrero.

"You win!" Proclaimed the man, "I can't force my pain onto others, I'll suffer your curse to protect my town." The dog smiled which was an odd and disturbing sight considering the kind of face it possessed at the moment.

"Are you sure?" asked the dog but the man just ignored him and made his way home. When he arrived something felt different, perhaps it was the new drapes, perhaps it was the fact that it was nearly dusk, or maybe, just maybe, it was the Chihuahua dressed in a sombrero and women's undergarments that stood at the door to his home, probably the drapes because they looked spectacular tonight. *What the in the name of... well this dog does he want now* thought the man along with some less than polite things he would enjoy doing to the supposed God.

"Choose," God spoke softly, "Be free of your curse and live a happy life with the experience I have given you or don't, I don't much care anymore"

"But why?" asked the man, "I thought you said you would make me keep the curse if I went home."

"A test," God told the man, "to see if you were a truly righteous and good willed person or not." In reality, that was only half the truth. The other half is that God was bored and needed somebody to screw with, so he chose the man as he was the epitome of average and needed something interesting in his life.

"Thank you" was all the man made out before the god vanished leaving behind a small box with the man's name engraved on it.

Curious the man opened the box to find a card with a single address written on it. *Nope* thought the man before throwing the card away and heading to bed to start his new life of freedom and retirement.

MEADOWLARK
A POEM BY: KENNEDY LANGLOIS

I cannot see in the dark
I cannot hear the meadowlark
I cannot hear the song it sings
The devil in my head, whispers
So many things.

Evil in my head he jeers
Echoed by demon cheers
Nails scratching through the night
Not an ear to listen to my plight

Bloody fingers scratch and bleed
He sneers and pays no merciful heed.
He puts his hands over my eyes
And whispers his plentiful lies

And it isn't as if I am blind
It's just that I've gone and lost my mind
For his sweet lies become my truth
And they work, corrupting my innocent youth.

SOFTEST WHISPER IN THE DARK
POEM BY: KENNEDY LANGLOIS

Softest whisper in the dark
That is what I am.
You hear me without listening
You see me without looking
You care without truly caring

Deepest shadow in the dark
That is what I am.
Right in front of you, yet hardly visible
A mountain to climb, yet you avoid
A shadow that you see out of the
Corner of your eye.
Not really there.
That is what I am.

MY FINAL DESTINATION
A SHORT STORY BY: GRACE COWTAN

When I finally push my way through the mass of people blocking the view to the outside, and directed my eyes upon the viewing port, I am awestruck.

The massive glowing orb, our final destination. At this distance, you could gaze upon her fertile soils, the pulsing veins of water running over her skin, and the vast blue oceans. This was the first time any of us had seen anything outside the Hexa5 and it was breath-taking.

My transmitter buzzed, and Sanchez's demanding voice sounded through slight static, "If you're done sightseeing, the captain has requested your presence in the Minor Bulkhead in thirty minutes."

Despite how much I hated Sanchez's filthy guts, I smile as I reach up to my earpiece to reply, "Will do."

20 minutes later I left the port and entered one of the many elevators that litters the Hexa5, traveling between the ships' many levels. The elevator engaged with a slight shake and began to move upwards.

The Hexa5 is big enough to cover at least ten football fields, and traversing its vast interior could take weeks. Part of our training included the memorization of the ships design, so we wouldn't get lost in our day-to-day activities. The ship could easily be compared to an old-style bees-nest. The largest levels are at the bottom, getting smaller as you go. The top of the ship is where the Minor Bulkhead is stationed.

I listen to the buzzing chatter of three newly-awoken Hexa-Citizens in the elevator as we rise gently past various floors through the hollow interior of the ship. Eventually the elevator sighs to a stop to release the three at the nutrition floor.

When the elevator gave out the light beeping that signaled I had reached my destination, I stepped to the door and placed my hand on the small white screening panel to be identified.

Entering the Bulkhead without being identified can result in the administering of an electric current being channeled throughout the interior of the elevator, rendering the intruder unconscious.

A light appeared on the panel underneath my palm, then the glass doors slid silently open to let me through. I cautiously stepped into the cool, blue-themed room. The walls appeared to be reflecting water, moving and pulsing just so it felt as if you were underwater, or on a beach back home, possibly drinking a Pina colada with a side of pineapple slices, watching the sun set.

My short fantasy was interrupted as Sanchez stepped out of a dark corner by the far wall, and came towards me. "The captain will be with us shortly, where are the others?"

"Others, sir?" I clear my throat and shift my gaze away, feeling intimidated. The elevator beeps then, releasing me from Sanchez' glare. I turn to see four individuals stride out of the elevator. The one in front, dressed in a blue, sterile-looking uniform, seemed the most confident, leading the group forward. The other three were less certain, keeping close together and were identical in their uniforms, which were white.

The captain emerges from a sliding glass panel that led to his private quarters, and smiles, "Welcome to the Bulkhead."

The captain isn't what most would think, instead of being an all-controlling, fear-inducing warlord, he actually has a small impact, only making an appearance on occasions like this, when a team was to head down to the surface.

I knew that along with these geeks, I was going to be touching alien soil. I couldn't come up with another reason why I would be summoned here.

The man in blue stepped forward, and extended a withered hand, wrinkled with age. "My name is Robin Mertz, and these are the individuals I've assembled, all are eager to be on this expedition, and to have Mr. Sanchez as our Squad leader."

I looked at the other three, one was shaking with...... Fear? Excitement? I couldn't tell.

Mertz continued, "This is my team," he gestured for them to step forward. "This is Rebecca Melbourne, Phillip Ward, and Todd Smith." All three shook the captain's hand.

The Captain took them in brusquely, then nodded approvingly. He nodded to Sanchez, who stood at attention, "A vesicle is being prepared for your departure and will be prepared to leave in three hours. I expect you will all be on it when it leaves." The captain nodded to the scientists, who thanked the captain and left, leaving me, as I hadn't been addressed. I was confused, until he dismissed Sanchez and turned to me. "Kerby Woods, I have been informed that a Photographic Specialist is to accompany the team down to the planet's surface, and so I have ordered for you to be suited up immediately. There is personnel waiting for you in the West Wing."

I had no idea where the west wing even started, but was saved from my ignorance when the captain buzzed in the prep team, and they lead me away. We did not take the elevator, but went down several flights of stairs, then entered a massive glass paneled corridor. The corridor echoed our footfalls, the sound ricocheting back and forth along the walkway. I was too excited to try and make conversation, and the stocky older man and mean-faced woman didn't look up to small talk at the moment, so I busied myself with looking out the transparent glass and into space.

I felt I would never get used to the feeling of insignificance at the sight of the planet. The solar system's sun made the planet glow as if it itself were alive, pulsing with energy. I could see the small pink moon, kaRla12, momentarily shielding the planet from the sun's rays as it passed. The second moon, just known as 'Tiny Tim', circled the planet more slowly.

The corridor ended, all too soon, and we enter several different rooms until we stop at a small, steel door. The man pulls out a small card, and slipped it into the screening panel, which beeped promptly. The door clicked, and the man pushed it open. Inside, the interior was hexagonally shaped. There were all sorts of gadgets lining the shelves, and the two-man prep-team promptly got to work. The woman walked over to a heavy-looking suit, and hefted it onto her shoulder, she reached into a shelf and pulled out several other pieces. She tossed the suit to me, then handed the small gadgets to the man.

"Put that on." She instructed. The man waited patiently for me to pull the suit on, then hooked the small tools to the collar.

Two hours later, I left the compartment and navigated my way out of the bulkhead region. With the help of a random citizen, I found the elevators that would take me directly to the Docking Bay.

The Bay is an odd area, not as large as one would expect but not too small either. It is a main large corridor with a higher ceiling, with small exit pods called 'Vesicles' pock-marking the entire thing.

By the time I hauled my equipment in and out of the elevators, and down to the awaiting vesicle, the team was already packed and was strapping into the pod. I quickly accommodate myself and gave short greeting to the team. I strapped in next to Mertz, dressed in heavy high-quality clothing. They all were, and Todd Smith was visibly puzzled as to what I was wearing.

"It's an Exo-suit," I explained, but before I could say more, Sanchez cleared his throat. "An Exo-suit is highly recommended for photographic pursuits, especially ones on alien planets." He smirked at me, then before anyone could say any more, Sanchez secured the airlock, spoke into his earpiece, and the detachment of the vesicle was commenced. A slight jolt was the evidence that we were no longer part of the ship. Small trinkets floated in the small space of the pod as we distanced ourselves from the Hexa5 and the artificial gravity was no more.

All was quite as we entered the atmosphere. The Pod port window began to light up from the blaze of the outer shell of the ship as the planet's gravity accepted us and pulled us downwards. The Pod jolted and my ears roared. My excitement was at its highest, and I couldn't stop smiling. After the Pod stopped shaking, Ward began to turn a pale white. There was another slight jolt; we were now secured to the Bio-dome.

The Bio-dome is a simple structure, but very large. It was built specifically for this expedition several weeks before the Hexa-citizens had been awoken from hyper-sleep. Its size is able to accommodate around fifty or more residents, but only a small team of around twenty building inspectors still reside in the dome, along with the staff that keep everything in order.

Sanchez secured the outer airlock remotely from a small screen at the doors of the pod, then opened the door. We were hasty to unload and see the interior of the dome. Melbourne and Smith was abuzz with exited chatter that I myself couldn't tune into to hear what they were saying. Ward looked a little green now as he slung a large pack over his shoulders, and I patted him on the back for reassurance.

It took all morning to tour the dome after we dropped off our supplies in our designated quarters. What I enjoyed the most was the greenhouse, and the coffee we had after was the best I ever had, as it had been grown her in the

Dome. Our quarters were located at the south curve of the Dome, opposite from were the main airlock was. The remaining team was situated in the upper levels and we wouldn't be seeing much of them after today, as Sanchez explained, they had a small gas leak in the Dome's main heating broiler which required many hands to fix.

When I was unpacking, Mertz came around to my door and knocked politely. I stood up. "Your names Kerby, right?" he asked. I nodded, "call me Woods," I shook his hand. "What's up?"

He cleared his throat, "Sanchez has called a meeting in the cafeteria, and it has something to do with an expedition."

"So soon? We've only been here for half a day though." I leaned past Hertz and out the doorway to see Melbourne leaving her room and walking down the hall to the cafeteria. Hertz just nodded.

We walked to the cafeteria together and when we pushed open the doors to the large dining room, Sanchez waved us over. He was already wrapping up the discussion with the rest of the team.

"How is he going to record *everything*? We could all do as good a job with individual helmet cameras." Smith was saying when we sat down. I realized they were taking about me. I piped up, "they equipped me with an Exo-suit, and it has built-in microfiber sensors that act as a tracking system, along with different styles of recording. You will all have individual cameras as well, but the Exo-suit is a higher advanced piece of hardware, so we are taking it for a test run."

Fifteen minutes later, Sanchez led the fully equipped team to the Airlock on the west side of the dome. I activated the Exo-suit with a series of vocal commands, and it hummed to life. The interior of the helmet lit up with small holographic lights that gave me a constant feed of stats from the team. Everything was either controlled by touch or by vocal command, no buttons protruded from either helmet or suit. The helmet was sturdy and clear, and I confidently entered the airlock. Our steel-bottomed boots clanged on the metal grating as we patiently waited for the chamber to pressurize. There was a hiss and the room filled with steam, then the signal gave out a shrill two-note sound as the outer doors opened with a groan. I step out behind Hertz and my boots crunched the rocky soil. My exhilarated breathing didn't fog up the helmet, as I surveyed the outside world surrounding us.

The outside of the dome was engulfed with various types of plantlike growth that had snaked out of the forest beyond. Smith reached out a heavily gloved hand and touched a leaf-like protrusion, which promptly turned brown and shriveled to a husk in his hand. Smith's mouth hung agape as he looked to Mertz in awe. Melbourne stood beside Smith and held a small device out into the growth. The device made a series of clicking noises, and Melbourne analyzed them. "These organisms aren't even carbon-based" she announced.

"What are they based from then?" Smith asked, dropping the leaf and looking over Melbourne's shoulder at the device.

"I honestly don't know, but I think this means that this planet probably has its own periodic table, just waiting to be discovered!"

Sanchez waited as the team reshuffled their packs into more comfortable positions before marching on into the 'forest'. We were heading towards a marker that was half a kilometer away from the dome. The canopy above us seemed empty save for the endless mass of trees and strange things protruding from the soil. Sanchez approached a large vine-like thing that had the thickness of a tree trunk, and prodded it with his rifle. The plant vibrated as if it were a mass of gelatin, sending reverberations high up into the canopy above. We stopped, all taken aback by the strange thing. Sanchez stepped back, but looked up the length of the vine with an angry scowl. He turned to us and motioned for us to continue on, clearly unimpressed with the scenery. Suddenly, a large glob of iridescent goo dropped down from above, and landed on his chest. He yelped and hurriedly scraped the oozing goo off of himself.

"What was that?" Sanchez growled to no one in particular.

"Maybe it was the trees?" I suggested half-heartedly.

Melbourne suggested we take a sample, and Sanchez denied her request and angrily pressed for us to keep up the pace as he waited to take the rear. We kept our eyes on the trees above, waiting to be hit by a ball of slime as we pressed forward.

Ten minutes into the trek, Melbourne stopped to take soil samples, and motioned for Smith to help her. Hertz hiked up his pack and approached a clump of small "shrubs" that glistened and jiggled as if they were made of Jell-O. Sanchez looked nervous still, and kept his sights on the forest for any sign of danger.

Ward twitched, as if he had been stung, and turned to me, "did you hear that?" His eyes darted around nervously. I look around, then check the Exo-suit's analyzer to see if it picked up any signal.

"The suit isn't picking up any outside signals, I'd say it was just your imagination." I assured Smith, and teasingly nudged his shoulder.

Melbourne and Smith stood, clearly done with their sample-taking. Several test-tubes clinked slightly as Smith gingerly put them back in the green bag he wore. Sanchez was pacing, impatiently. Ward didn't seem convinced and gave off obvious nervous energy as we start off once again. Several paces in, Sanchez called from the rear, "Hold up! I thought I heard something."

Ward and I exchanged glances. We stopped, and listened. Suddenly a shrill sound pierced through the thick atmosphere, drilling into our helmets and making our ears ring. Sanchez suddenly lost it, "Alright, I've had enough of this! Let's turn back."

We made back the way we came, just as the canopy above started to sway violently, as if there were a gang of alien-orangutans, swinging through the gelatinous branches above us. Drops of ooze splattered down from above, covering us almost completely with slime, and made running very difficult. With Smith in the lead, we exited a thick patch of vegetation and entered a small clearing.

Melbourne turned and looked around frantically, "Where is Sanchez? He was right behind me a minute ago!"

We all stop and look back into the dark recession of the iridescent growth for any signs of Sanchez. The trees stop swaying.

"Sanchez!"

"Sanchez, were the hell are you?!"

"Stop messing around!"

Our calls turn up no reply, and I knew that, somehow, those things had taken him. "Should we go find him?" Melbourne said uncertainly.

I shook my head solemnly. That's when the forest erupted in a massive cacophony of shrill whistles and clicks, drowning out everything. The noise reminded me of a pack of wild animals that had just made a kill.

"Move!!" Ward screamed, and we bolted back to the dome. As we ran, it became harder to move my limbs, and I noticed the trees were shaking again, violently showering us with the thick slime.

"Oh God," Melbourne kept repeating, until we could see the glow of the Bio-Dome's lights.

Before we reached the outer airlock doors, I transmitted to the team inside, "This is the excursion team! There's something in the forest! They took Sanchez!" I quit blabbering, "Unlock the outer doors!" Oddly, I got only static in return.

Ward scrabbled at the doors, trying in vain to get them open. "They are locked Ward! Only the team inside can open them," I announced, and the team looked at me, afraid.

"They would know we are here, there are sensors that surround the dome." Smith said, checking the outer airlock doors now along with Ward.

"They didn't receive my transmission," I announced, telling the two that their efforts were futile.

Suddenly, off in the distance, a deep whirring brought our attention to the other airlock on the south side of the Dome, facing the setting sun. I realized it was the Shuttle, and someone was warming the engines. They were leaving us.

"What's going on Mertz?" I shouted over the increasing volume of the Shuttles roaring engines. I was unable to hide the terror in my voice. Mertz looked at me, equally afraid, and shook his head.

The whirr became a booming roar, and the shuttles engines activated, sending a plume of gas into the evening air. It detached from the airlock and we watched in stunned silence as it became a speck in the hazy clouds, then disappeared altogether.

We stood there, forgetting the danger surrounding us. The silence was broken by Smith's crying.

"I hate to say this, but we are dead men." Ward says, his eyes look to the sky, then slowly come to rest on each of us.

"Why would they leave us here?" Melbourne asks, taking off her pack and letting it fall to the ground.

"What if this was all planned? That would be a good explanation as to why the airlocks won't open!" Smith blubbered, slowly becoming more crazed.

"Shut up! They wouldn't play games with us like that! Get a hold on yourself." I almost shout, my anger rising, "They wouldn't do that to us"

"Why else would they send *you* down here? All suited up with all that recording hardware?" The video feed is probably streaming back up to the Hexa5 right now, and I'll tell you, what a show it would be for them!"

Mertz stepped in, and slapped Smith across the face. Smith stopped, and seemed to come out of his stupor. Mertz turned to the rest of us, standing in silence for a moment, "I think we should go back, to look for Sanchez's weapon. It may be the difference between life and death now."

"I'm not going, no way am I going back in *there*." Smith whimpered, then curled up beside the Dome.

"We should stick together, Smith, what if those things come back and you're here all alone?" Melbourne said in an even tone, then knelt down beside him.

Smith shook his head in protest. I look to ward, and we nod our heads in silent agreement. We leave him here.

Evidence of the setting sun showed as a bright pink line on the horizon, and on the large towering tree-like vegetation as it glistened on the gel like leaves. We kept our distance from the growth as we trudged warily on to the place were Sanchez went missing.

Several minutes passed in silence until Ward, in the front, stopped suddenly. He stepped back, while Mertz stepped forward.

"What is it?" I call from behind Melbourne.

"Its bones," Mertz motions me forward, and I go up to look.

In a small, neat little pile, a whole human skeleton has been discarded, and when I kick aside a femur, the skull is revealed. It glared at us with hollow eye sockets and gapped with clean white teeth.

"This must be Sanchez." I look at Mertz, and he nervously scratched his shoulder.

"Those things that took him must be composed of some sort of acid," Melbourne suggests solemnly, stepping forward. "Must have ate him whole." She stepped reached down and carefully moved the skull to the side, then pulled out a gnarled, acid-pocked object.

"Oh no," she dropped the lump of metal. Mertz and Ward exchanged glances.

It was Sanchez's gun.

An urgent beeping sound made everyone jump. I realize it was from the Exo-suit. The screen inside my helmet showed that Smiths stats had stopped coming in.

"Something happened to Smith," I informed everyone.

"That means those things are at the Bio Dome",
Melbourne whispered, covering her helmet with
shaking hands.

I heard a sharp, whistle-like clicking behind me,
looks of horror overcome the faces of my team.

Then I realized that the creatures were not at the
Dome, they were here, surrounding us from all
directions, sliding and oozing from the forest,
dripping slime onto us from above. The thick, hot
ooze enveloped everything around us. Slowly,
puddles of the iridescent slime came together and
formed into larger beings, almost as tall as a man.
We watched as bubbles formed inside the
substance, creating the clicking, popping, whistling
sounds when they rose to the surface and burst.
They formed a tight circle, seven masses pressing
in from all sides, and we were running out of room
fast.

They trapped us with no escape. The slimy
beings looked alive, bubbles forming and popping
so quickly they seemed to be boiling. The noise was
deafening, the sharp whistling of the pack
reminded me once again of animals about to make
a kill. The sound grew louder and louder still as
they drew inwards, closer and closer, until they
merged together and the slime became one. It was
now a giant seething mass, with us engulfed inside
it.

I could not move, the Exo-suit was completely seized. A feeling of pure dread washed over me, knowing now that there was absolutely no escape, everyone was completely immobilized.

This is it, my final destination. In the belly of the unknown, being digested alive along with my human comrades. I close my eyes and wait for the dark.

Death is interrupted, a vision appears on the back of my eyelids. I see a mass of "trees", large, towering things that seemed to be located in one large area of the forest. From these tree hang sacks of translucent globs, like large grapes, or maybe eggs. Surrounding the sacks, like protective guardians, are hundreds of the slime forms.

I get it then, it was their nesting grounds, if things such as these could even nest.

The sight changes, and an image of the Bio-Dome is superimposed onto where the grounds were. They lost their young to the erecting of the Dome. The image morphs again, still the Bio-Dome, but now with a layer of acidic slime covering every surface of it. The dome steamed as the acid burned through. In part of the image, I see the Shuttle leaving. That is why they left?

The image fades to black, and stars dance behind my lids.

The heaviness of my limbs subsides, and I am able to move the suit up into a sitting position. I open my eyes, and I am surrounded by bones. Clean, white skulls gape at me, forever in an expression of horror. I assess the damage, and notice that the Exo-suit is pock-marked with acid stains. They tried to get me, but they failed and gave me a message instead. I look around, and notice that the sun had gone down, and in the sky I see two moons, casting the ghostly light upon the boneyard. The forest is barren, the beings had gone.

I am alone with the skeletons.

The only thing I can think of is leaving, and I stand, then start to walk back the way I came.

This is my final destination.

REVENGE OF THE ORPHAN
A SHORT STORY BY: EMMA NAPIER

The day was chilly. The wind stung her skin like
thousands of tiny razors. The leaves cascaded
down, carried by the wind. It smelled of musty
leaves, yet somehow the night was welcoming.

Stacy was completely at peace as she strolled
down the deserted street. She had always liked
being alone and felt as though that was when she
was most thoughtful. She was a beautiful girl, and
what little friends she had would describe her as a
little bit crazy sometimes. She was a good person in
the sense that she went to church and always put
money in the boxes by the till. Her upbringing had
been tragic and she had grown up an orphan,
though that had never stopped her from being a
good citizen. She was walking home alone after her
shift at the diner.

What Stacy did not know yet, was she was not
completely alone. Behind her followed a man in all
black attire, blending into the night, stealthier than
a jungle cat stalking its prey. It seemed as though
that was exactly what he was doing; stalking his
prey. He intently focused on his mission, he was so
infatuated with Stacy that he did not see the
garbage bin in front of him and knocked it over.
Quickly he ducked behind a nearby car. But he was
not quick enough.

Stacy saw the shadow man behind her, she grew scared quickly. She knew that if he had been an innocent person he would not have tried to hide. She decided not to run, so instead she dialed her friend up on her phone. She was soon to be home anyways and she would consider calling the police then. She tried not to let the person following her realize she knew he was there. She walked at a normal pace and tried to keep her breathing and conversation normal. Stacy figured that this person was going to follow her home so she decided to invite her friend over for drinks. She assumed no one would stick around if someone was with her.

As soon as Stacy stepped in the door she started to lock every single door and window she had. She closed all her curtains and turned on all her lights. She was slightly out of breath by the time she finished, she took a moment to collect herself.

"Protection." Stacy thought.

Quickly she walked into the kitchen to grab the biggest knife she could along with some loose pepper flakes.

Just as she finished pouring the pepper into a bag, the doorbell went.

"Be cautious but not weird," Stacy told herself in order to stay calm. She knew it was her friend, though her wild imagination thought that it was her stalker, here to take her to a dirty rancid basement in which she would die. She held the knife behind her back and checked the peephole. With a sigh of relief she opened the door.

"Mary! It's so great to see you!" Stacy exclaimed a little too happy.

"Yeah… Are you okay?" Mary questioned as Stacy pulled her into the room and shut and locked the door behind her.

"Yes, yes, I'm alright, can never be too careful you know? What with all the weirdos running around these days."

"No, I guess you can't be…" Mary was still unconvinced, "Are you sure there's nothing wrong? You're acting a little paranoid. What's bothering you?"

"Oh it's nothing, I suppose I'm just being a little silly bu-"

"Stacy why do you have that knife?"

"I was cooking. When you came here I was chopping up some fruit. I would be a terrible hostess if I did not have some snacks for us to munch on wouldn't I?" Stacy said a little too quickly.

"Right, okay. I brought a movie."

"Which one?" Stacy called from the kitchen.

"The Strangers." Said Mary, using a spooky voice to emphasize that it was a horror movie.

Stacy grabbed the snacks and a blanket and headed to the couch to watch the movie. It was a scary movie and more unusual then most, but

Stacy was not really paying attention, she was looking at all the windows and doors and thinking of all the vulnerable places her house had.

She decided that she was going to find out who this guy was and what he wanted. She did not want to be another statistic. She was going to do what her daddy used to tell her to, "When the world gets tough, you get tougher."

When Stacy woke up Mary was long gone and had left a note that read, "Stacy, got called into work, had a great time last night. P.S, there's some creep walking up and down the street."

Stacy got shivers when reading the last part. She knew this meant he knew where she lived, and was watching her every move. She knew this meant she had to act as though nothing was bothering her. Stacy would have to continue life as normal. Then tonight, she would find out where he lived.

Stacy proceeded through the day slightly paranoid, he followed her to the store, her workplace, and back home again. He was still standing outside as the sun was setting. He thought she could not see him through the shrub he stood behind. He could not be more wrong. Stacy went around the house closing any blinds that would allow him to see her sneak out. She went to her room, put leggings and a black hoodie on, and tucked her hair into a baseball cap. She then crawled on her hands and knees to the back door, so as not to let him spot her. She knew that soon he would become bored and leave her home, only to lead her right to his. She was going to find anything to tell her who he was, anything that would help her report him to the police.

As Stacy walked around the block he saw her coming, he began to walk away from her house as he tried to look innocent, Stacy knew he was not.

She followed him for about 20 minutes, by then it was completely dark, she was very wary about where he was going. Stacy knew it was possible he knew she was following him, and was trying to lure her into a trap. Anytime he walked through a dark alley or a desolate park, Stacy took the scenic route, knowing she would always catch up to him, as he moved awful slow for a stalker.

Stacy herself had become quite good at finding things to hide behind, and knew her slender figure was an advantage. She dodged this way and that making sure she was a respectable length behind.

As Stacy dove toward a tree for cover, she caught her foot on a tree root, twisting her ankle. Silently, she cussed, trying not to make a sound. She grabbed her foot for a second. She then released it and tried to put some pressure on it.

Stacy cried out as her foot touched the ground, quickly covering her mouth and waiting a moment to hear the inevitable footsteps coming her way. Thankfully that never happened.

She knew she could not continue like this, but she had come too far to give up. Stacy did not know much about the medical field, she was a magazine editor for goodness sakes. However Stacy did remember something her mother told her about wrapping up sore limbs, with that thought, she took out the pocket knife she had brought along for protection, and cut a long strip of her sweater off. She tried to move fast but gingerly as she did not want to lose her stalker, she wrapped her ankle in the makeshift tenser bandage, then used a bobby pin to hold it together.

Stacy got back to her feet and tested the foot once again, it hurt still, but the pain was manageable. She poked her head out from behind the tree and did a victory dance inside her head. He was very far ahead but she could still see him. It was much harder to be stealthy with her injured ankle, though she was making good progress, soon she caught up. She took slow precise steps now, careful not to crunch leaves.

They were now going on 30 minutes of walking, Stacy was getting tired and her injured foot was not helping. Somewhere in the next 5 minutes, they came to an abrupt stop. They now were standing in front of a dark scary forest. It loomed over the both of them, this is exactly what you would expect to see in a horror movie. Crows cawed from within, warning the outsiders of the danger that lay inside.

With only a slight hesitation, the man walked inside and drudged along a small, slightly beaten down trail.

Stacy knew better than to follow him in. She sat a few minutes and weighed her options. It was late, Stacy did not want all of this work to have been for nothing. Although at the same time, it would have all been for nothing if she were to have gotten herself caught. She could call the police but at this point she had done as much bad as he had. However, Stacy had figured that her intentions were more pure than his. That would not matter to the police though.

Soon enough, Stacy came to the conclusion that she had lived a good life, and that even if she went home now, he could still come back and harm her. She knew this was the only way to end this. So Stacy stood up and stretched her muscles out, letting a few joints crack. Surreptitious people did not have bones cracking when doing their dirty work. Once she was sure she was good to go, she bravely walked into the forest. It was colder in here than out in the open. Probably because of how dense it was. Stacy clenched her jaw in order to prevent her teeth from chattering. Just in case he was nearby. The fabric missing from her sweater did not help her problem either. She was so cold and the trail seemed to go for miles.

One more step. She would tell herself, it cannot be too much farther.

She continued on for 15 minutes. Each step she took, feeling a little more discouraging. Then there was a light. At the lowest point of a valley that had seemed to appear out of nowhere, there was a light. It was not very big, you almost had to squint to see it. It was not very bright either, though it had a soft yellow glow that seemed welcoming.

Against her better judgement Stacy quickly but carefully hurried toward the light, hoping it would offer warmth. She made every step scrupulously, so as not to aggravate her injury, or worse yet, go tumbling down the hill and obtain more injuries. As Stacy walked down, the light grew bigger and brighter, still staying a warm yellow. About halfway down, she could make out the shape of an old, unsturdy cabin. The light emanated from a window in the cabin, inside she could see a shadow or two, moving about.

Stacy tiptoed her way to the cabin crouching lower and lower as she came closer and closer. This was it, the home of her stalker. Her heart was beating really fast as she looked for a way in. Obviously she opted for the front door, but realized it was not an option when she gingerly placed a foot on it and it creaked into the night. She snuck around the side, sticking as close as she could to the old cabin, keeping in mind that his whereabouts inside, were completely unknown. Stacy saw a backdoor and almost gasped when she saw the man on the back porch with a cigarette hanging out of his mouth. She knew at that moment her route in and out, and she knew she had a very small amount of time to get what she was looking for.

Quickly she headed to the other side and jimmied the window open. Stacy hoisted herself up, being much louder than she had hoped for. The inside was much more normal than you would think, dare she say, cozy? Stacy had not a second to admire it though she knew that she would be caught if she was not in and out in a heartbeat. She looked around for anything that could identify him. A quick scan of the room showed that an old rickety desk with a stack of papers was her best bet. She walked over and shuffled through them. A few papers through and no useful information was found. Until she stumbled upon a piece of mail, addressed to a Samuel Admeer.

Stacy gasped and dropped it. This was not possible, he was gone. He disappeared after he killed her mom.

Stacy's thoughts were broken as she heard a throat clear behind her. She froze and slowly turned around to see the only person she'd ever hated with every piece of her soul. Her heart was beating so fast she thought it might explode her chest. Her mouth was dry and her palms sweaty. Her jaw was clenched as she tried not to scream out.

"My beautiful daughter, it's so great to see you again. It's been what? 15 years would you say?"

Stacy tried to respond calmly, "About that, yes." Her voice could cut through bricks.

"I have to say you definitely acquired some of my skill. It couldn't have been easy to find me here." There was slight amusement in his voice, "I've been watching you for a couple years now. Hoping that you would see things from my perspective. Hoping you would join me. Being a criminal is quite fun you know. And you get to change your look all the time. You're never the same person, but you're always you. Do you get what I mean by that."

Stacy was hoping her face was neutral, this situation did not look good for her. She was backed up against the desk and was fidgeting with something on it that was behind her back. After a moment she responded, "I missed you."

He looked surprised for a moment, but soon after released a maniacal laugh.

"People always told me you were more like me then your mother."

Stacy held back a cringe and faked a smile, "Yes people told me that too."

"Look at us being so formal," he said, "come give me a hug."

Stacy moved a couple steps forward to meet him and felt somewhat safe in his embrace. She smiled and brought her hand up, she felt him cough and his body get heavy. She stepped back to admire the sight of him slump to the floor in a pool of his blood. His eyes were opened wider than she thought possible and he gripped at the letter opener in the side of his neck.

He gave it a tug and as it came out the pool of crimson blood now surrounding him grew bigger.

Stacy just stood there and smiled as she watched the puddle grow bigger and his life grow less. She got on her knees beside him and leaned down to his ear.

"For mother." She whispered, and plunged the weapon into his neck once more.

DUST

AN HONORABLE MENTION STORY BY: LAYTON GUISE

Prologue

Hello, this is agent 863 of the Australian Armed Forces (AFF), call sign "Coyote". I am filing this report, not only to my family, but to my commanding officer… the mission was a failure. I found the warhead in the center of Perth, Australia, but was unable to disarm in time. Two million people are dead, and it is because of me. The radiation will soon take my life, either that, or the warped distorted creatures created by said radiation. This is "Coyote" signing off.

Clark always despised that call sign, but it had been his nickname since he had enlisted into the AAF. This would be his seventh year in the military, and unfortunately his last, he had known too much, and would be branded a traitor to his country. At the prime age of eighteen, Clark had signed up before he had even finished high school, ditching his old life for a chance to fight for his country.

Despite the fact that he was so young, the AAF accepted him regardless, they were desperate for soldiers, especially ones in such flawless shape. Clark was always the envy of other men, he stood at 6'5", with rich delicate, jet black hair, and a body lined with rough muscles. Calling him a fighter would be a harsh insult, the man was tougher than nails, and stronger than concrete, but nothing would prepare him for what had happened….

What Australia had suffered was a perfect example of how little humanity trusted each other, throwing morals and politics out the window. Once the Aussies had uncovered the element nicknamed "Supermetal", sh** hit the fan. The UN had disbanded that day and the Australian Government unveiled the first Supermetal sample to the world, and all-out war began. The USA spear-headed the invasion, allying with Europe, and wasting no time invading us.

Only having a few weeks to prepare, we rapidly harvested and manufactured weapons using Supermetal, one of which, was the Goliath M1 Mechanized Assault Suit, also known as the Goliath M1 MAS. That was the suit Clark was stuck inside, and the desperate struggle to escape had begun.

The emergency escape hatch would not budge, damned Russians had set up Anti-tank mines all around the city. This left me no choice but to sit tight and wait, and of course, the radiation has blocked radio communications, leaving me as a sitting duck. It has already been three hours, and the sun is near setting.

The Russians will likely be back soon, like the vultures they are, and I refuse to go down without a fight. My orders say that if any enemies are in a position to capture any functioning Supermetal, I must self-destruct the Goliath. Killing any attackers in the process. Until this happens though, I might as well get some sleep, it is going to be a long night.

As Clark drifted off to sleep, he began to recount several memories from earlier in his life, some were significant events, and others were not. One, to be specific, was the reason he signed up for the military.

Graduation was only a month away when it happened, Clark's girlfriend Stacy has recently become incredibly depressed, and it was no secret why.

Stacy's father had died. Killed in a grocery store shooting a week prior, she was beyond devastated. She had spent all her time in her room, refusing to eat, or talk to anyone but Clark. He told her all the time how special she was to him. He brought her gifts, spent time with her, and watched movies with her, but it was not enough. The day of their anniversary, Clark had entered her room for the final time, his arms full of flowers, chocolates and movies, only to find Stacy, dead.

She had used her father's rifle to kill herself, her suicide note detailed her final thoughts. Clark could not bring himself to read it, he was already in tears. Stacy's mom and younger brother were watching the whole scene unfold, mouths agape. He could not stand to see it anymore. Clark left Stacy's family to grieve, and on his way out, he heard another gunshot from the house, followed by a young boy's screams. He would never forget, he never could forget, and he would remember that night until the day he breathed his last.

As the dream began to fade out, his ears began to pick up a soft scratching noise, it began to get progressively louder, filling his ear drums. Until it suddenly stopped, and three exact seconds passed, before it broke through...

It had breached the armored suit, and although he could not see the beast, but he knew exactly what he was dealing with. There was not a name for it, but the radiation due to the bombings in Perth and the surrounding area, had mutated all of the animals and bugs within it. Nothing but distorted beasts and monsters in the place of its once thriving citizens. The creature stood at nine feet tall, the same size as his suit, but its claws were six times the size of swords, and twenty times as sharp, it was going to kill him. He could feel his heart rate climbing.

Clark reached for anything to fend the creature off, only securing a low caliber pistol. Naturally, he had stored his larger firearm outside his suit, not expecting something to break in. Now was not the time to give up though. He scanned the creature's vile claws, attempting to find a weak spot, only locating a stray vein.

"F*** it," he whispered to himself, as twelve rounds explode out of the small pistol and towards the exposed vein.

It worked. The creature releases a primal screech so loud it forces him to cover his ears, it draws its arm from the suit, but not before lunging forward. Impaling Clark on one of its massive claws. Blood rapidly escapes his wound as he makes a feeble attempt to cover it, and now his vision was beginning to blur. He hears the creature scream again, but another more hopeful noise fills the air as well.

It is the sound of gunfire. He listens to a couple thousand rounds get poured into the beast, before an explosion is heard, and the ground quakes as the creature finally breathes its last. The air is now silent, and he hears boots approaching his suit. Unsure of what side they are on, he exits through the hole the beast made, and waves his hands in the air desperately. The men stop in their tracks and aim their weapons at me, and begin to speak to themselves… in Russian.

His hands drop to his sides and he turns around, the Russians get progressively louder, shouting and begin to fire shots into the air. He dives around to the back of the suit, so they can no longer see him and he opens up a keypad. The keypad is the one to his weapon and he begins to type in his password. When he does this, he remembers her, but wipes the thoughts from his memory, he has to be strong for this.

He opens the hatch, and unstraps the large caliber rifle, and proceeds towards the second keypad, the one that can self-destruct the Goliath and he begins typing in the second password. This one is less emotional, but he can still feel the butterflies swarming inside him. He is afraid to meet her again. He grips his weapon and circles around to the other side of the suit after arming the core, and at this point the Russians are only ten feet away, unprepared for his attack.

He has a minute and forty-five seconds left until the suit detonates, and a minute and forty-five seconds to kill these bastards. He has ten of them in his view and immediately fires on the one in the back, hitting him squarely in the chest, not killing him but knocking the wind out of him. Annoyed, he fires three more shots, two of them at his neck, the final in his jaw. *"Good enough."* At this point, the other nine have Clark in their sights and begin firing panicked and sloppy shots towards him, too afraid to stop and line up a proper shot.

He has thirty-six rounds remaining. He fires two more into the enemy at the very front, one misses his head by a centimeter and the second goes straight through his eye and out of the back of his skull. There are eight remaining. They now begin to group up, and are trying to carry off the wounded soldiers, that was their mistake. He finds the two soldiers carrying off the wounded, and fires on their exposed backs, hitting them both in the spine but expends four bullets to do so. There are only five remaining, but it is at this point that one of them gets lucky, and lands a hit on Clarks right kneecap.

He cannot help but wretch in pain as the shards of bone act like puny daggers, stabbing everywhere into his leg. He attempts to stand, but cannot, knowing this, he crawls towards an opening, desperately searching for a shot. He finds one, and takes note of how quickly and confidently they are approaching him. *"Time to punish them"* They are only five feet away at this point, and he has thirty rounds remaining. He unloads his remaining magazine onto the soldiers' surprised faces.

Twenty eight rounds fired, ten of them missed, and the remaining eighteen were enough to tear the five men apart, leaving twitching corpses in their place.

He has two rounds, and thirty one seconds before the Supermetal core detonates, but a new threat approaches. He had forgotten completely about the other six men, as they circled around him and now attempt to disarm the Goliath core. Their weapons are strewn across the ground, and they all have desperate looks plastered across their faces. They finally notice him and stop, it feels like time stood still for a moment.

He has two rounds for six men, how is he going to figure this one out? He considers his options. He has three… he can either shoot two of the men, shoot the core, or shoot himself. He has twenty one seconds remaining.

He stares at the Russian men straight in the eyes, and points his rifle at them, they are at an impasse. They do not have the guts to try and grab their weapons, and he is not going to waste his final two rounds. Fifteen seconds remain.

He notices that several Russian aircraft and land vehicles are approaching the scene. Eleven seconds remain.

He looks up at the core, and notices it is growing increasingly unstable. Four seconds remain.

He puts his finger on the trigger of his rifle, and aims it upward. At this point the six remaining men begin running and frantically shouting at their comrades to flee.

It is too late for that. Two seconds remain. He thinks one last time of his family, his friends and her, and a single tear escapes his eye – he pulls the trigger. One second remained, as the core finally detonated.

The city of Perth was no more, as the Supermetal core created an explosion eighty seven thousand times that of an atomic warhead. Leaving nothing but radiation and rubble, but something managed to survive. It was Clark.

You would not have known that by looking at him. The unbelievable amounts of radiation had let him survive for what would be his final moments.

Am I thinking? Am I even alive? Well of course I am, but for how long? I have nothing left, no organs, no eyes, no hair, nothing. Is this radiation keeping me alive? Why? Is this punishment for deciding to live, instead of taking my own life that evening? She had loaded two rounds into the rifle. She planned on me joining her, in whatever afterlife existed, but instead I decided to kill people. I killed people with families, and lives, but I did not care, I wanted revenge.

I try to cry, but the radiation has melted off my tear ducts. Hallucinations begin to invade my sight, as I see people, innocent people, being melted to the bone from this radiation.

Why me? Who do I have to suffer this pain for any longer? God continues to tease me, I just want to see her one final time before I leave this hell-like existence.

His final plea was heard, as he sees her, atop a hill of dust, calling his name, over and over again. His dying walk turns into a painful run, as he desperately scales the dust mountain, and finally reaches her.

She is as beautiful as ever, and they stare into each other's eyes for what seems like a millennium. The reflection in her watery blue pupils is one of happiness, enthusiasm, and life. Nothing lasts forever though, especially happiness. The darkness of reality seeps in, as she meets the same fate as Clark would. Her beautiful eyes now melt into her skull, and she begins to feel the effects of the radiation as Clark had, until there was nothing left of his once beautiful woman.

Clark felt himself finally leaving this existence behind, God had had his fun with him, and it is about time he sent Clark spiraling into what would be his final fate: hell.

As the moon finally rose into the sky again that night, it shone its light onto the dust that was the city of Perth, and not a soul survived.

Made in the USA
Columbia, SC
18 June 2017